SIREN

BOOK 3 OF THE VUKASIN SAGA

B.D. Snowden

GEEKY GOTH PRESS

DEDICATION

This book is dedicated to the guys and dolls of Frank & Joe's Coffee House who kept the caffeine flowing while I finished writing during a turbulent time in my life.

ACKNOWLEDGMENTS

As always the men and women of Books, Booze, and Betas kept me motivated and inspired.   I am grateful to my family who are being supportive in my decision to write full time. Thank you for taking this leap of faith with me.

CHAPTER ONE

They threw his bloodied and broken body into the cell. He was a man again having lost consciousness after battling dozens of opponents at once. The jostling of the guards woke him up once more. As soon as his feet hit the floor he charged the guards pouring into what he considered his lair. Six of them hit him with their stun sticks. It was a point of pride that he was up to six. It had started as only one guard stunning him when they had brought him here who knows how many months ago. He had killed that guard. They steadily increased the number to try and control him; but they could never control him. They could only cage him.

He wasn't just a monster; he was the most feared monster in a menagerie of monsters. He shifted into his phased form, the beast within that Vukasin warriors called upon in the heat of battle. He spent more and more time as the beast rather than the man. He would have forgotten that his name was Akia of the clan Tiaret, if he didn't use that information as a mantra to remind him of the man he used to be. Akia had no place in the fight rings and by extension he had no place in the gladiator slave cells either. The one who resided here was known as the Vukasin Beast.

Akia slammed into the guards throwing them against the stone walls of his prison. Those that could quickly scrambled to get out of the cell. Those that could not looked on in horror as Akia viciously beat their comrades to death before turning his fury onto them. The guards who could ran out of the cell and slammed the cell door closed leaving their doomed brethren behind. They engaged the locks as the beast howled and raged within.

Each day it seemed it was harder and harder to return to the man. Little by little the beast was winning. Akia didn't know how much longer he would be able to hold out before letting the beast inside him take over. He despaired of ever being free. At this point even if he was free he would probably be more of a danger to his loved ones. Perhaps it was best if he was kept caged until his death.

Akia prowled in the beast's body but his mind turned to memories of his past, when he was still more man than beast. He didn't regret sacrificing his freedom for that of his brother. He had seen how his brother had held the little human woman like she was a precious treasure. He had read in his twin's mind how much he had come to care for her in such a short time. With both of them free he hoped that his brother had been able to stake his claim. If his reckoning was correct it had been nearly a year since they had been in the valley prison together. It was possible that Banji might even have a whelp by now. Akia would like to think that was the case. His brother happy with a family made this hell worth it.

Akia tried to concentrate on pushing the beast back into his mental cage. He was finding it harder and harder to revert back to a man after the adrenaline rush of battle. Each day he was pitted against more vicious and stronger opponents. It would be easy to let one of them kill him, but his beast's survival instincts were just too strong. Besides the man in him wasn't quite ready to die just yet. He still had some unfinished business.

Then he heard it. A sound so pure and beautiful that you couldn't help stopping to listen. It was a voice that captured you in a magic spell and transported you to someplace else. That beautiful siren call was the one thing that calmed the raging beast within him. Akia listened to her every night; she didn't know it but she was his lifeline to his sanity. Without her the beast would have won long ago.

Tonight her song was melancholic. It pulled at the darkest sadness within one's psyche and brought it to the surface until it was spilling out down your cheeks. Akia couldn't understand the language the woman sang in, but every emotion brushed against his soul. Every night her voice rescued him and gave him one more day where the beast didn't win.

Slowly Akia's body changed and contorted. The fangs that filled his mouth receded back to a man's bite. His body rippled as his great pelt of fur disappeared leaving behind scarred skin. He might still carry his brother's face, but their bodies were vastly different now. The midnight blue eyes were still clear, but somehow harder than they once had been. His serious personality had been replaced with a brutality he hadn't known he had possessed. His dark hair lay in shaggy lanks to his shoulders instead of the close and neat military cut he once favored. His body was even more impressively muscled than it had been. His trained warrior's physique honed in the fires of hell.

Akia collapsed into an exhausted heap. The few comforts once afforded to the gladiators enslaved here had long ago been removed from his cell. His guards had learned the hard way that he was willing to turn anything into a weapon.

Akia rolled his battered body over. He needed sleep before they came for him again. He closed his eyes and let his spirit float away to the mystical tones of his mystery woman. He vowed he would stay alive long enough to see her free.

*****

Days and nights blurred into each other. He fought, he won, and then the guards would wrestle the beast back into his cell. More and more frequently they forced medical care onto him after the battle in the arena. He only returned to a man with the song of his unknown siren, whose music was becoming darker and filled with sadness and despair. Even as it ripped his emotions apart, her song still quieted the beast.

Once more they tossed the battered beast into the cell. The guards this time were using the new pulse shields to protect themselves. The beast smiled at the thought that they were developed just because of him. While it kept his claws from shredding them, he quickly discovered that a powerful hit would send them reeling. So he did what he did in the gladiatorial arena: he adapted his fighting strategy.

Akia charged at the men hitting their shields with the full force of a rhino-bear. The kinetic energy then transferred to the guard holding the shielding device. At least two guards had the bones in their arms snap. One guard flew across the room and hit the stone wall with a sickening crunch. Akia's keen eye discovered that they had to momentarily lower their shields to hit him with the stun stick or a pulse gun.

Akia had been hit so many times with stunning weapons that unless he was hit with multiple weapons at the same time, they did little more than annoy him. But his annoyance gave him the opening he needed to grab the throat of one guard and snap his neck. The rest descended into chaos when they realized he had already discovered the weakness in their new defense.

Akia chuckled, which sounded more like a dog panting in his phased form. Terrorizing his guards was becoming too easy. That was the beast in him talking; the one who reveled in the pain of others to prove his dominance. He had the last unfortunate guard pinned to the ground and was slowly squeezing the life out of him. This guard had attempted to phase into his own battle beast and meet him head on. Despite the strength enhancing drugs the Tanis Clan used to control their soldiers, the guard didn't stand a chance, even with an injured Akia. The beast enjoyed seeing the terror and then acceptance in the man's eyes. When the life left his eyes, the guard's body shifted back to that of a man. Akia briefly wondered whether he would shift back when he died or would he remain a beast forever?

"Ahm." Akia turned to face the new threat. The man he wanted to kill more than any other was standing in the doorway of his cell - Daemon Tanis, the casino king of the Tanis scourge, second in wealth and influence only to Bel the false *Khalon* of the Tanis clan. He had crawled his way up the ranks as an elite soldier. Even his loss to Megan before the *Mate Avi Keiger* hadn't slowed his ambition. This man was a true sadist and he was the man who kept the beast caged.

Daemon Tanis, the bastard who controlled the fight rings, would have killed him long ago if he hadn't proven to be so profitable. Which was why that piece of dragon-spider shit wanted him alive and healthy. The ritual was the same. Akia was thrown into the battle ring to entertain the indolent rich with death and destruction. When he vanquished those poor souls and creatures pitted against him, he was dragged back to his cell and a medic was sent to treat his wounds. Daemon wanted to make sure his credit maker was hale and hearty for the next fight.

When Akia had discovered that the medics weren't just seeing to his wounds but injecting drugs meant to bring his phased state to the surface and increase his savagery and strength, he began maiming and killing them as well. They were the enemy, as they were men who sided with the scum known as Tanis. But Daemon was a clever bastard and soon started using the delicate and fragile women enslaved on this backwater planet to treat him. The beast in him may take over completely one day, but for now Akia retained enough control not to physically harm the women that were imprisoned as much as he was. He did still retain some honor. He did however scare them enough that he heard the guards talking about the fact that the women refused to come back even with the threat of torture.

Akia howled in triumph. He had finally forced Daemon to deal with him face-to-face. He would probably die in the attempt to kill his enemy, but it gave him the opportunity to take out the bastard. Akia crouched on all fours like the beast trying to take over his mind and sprang toward Daemon. The man's self-satisfied smirk further inflamed the rage burning in Akia's soul.

Akia raised one clawed hand in preparation to shred Daemon's body apart. As his sharp talons descended, Daemon yanked a woman that Akia hadn't noticed in front of him. No wonder the bastard was smirking.

The woman watched Akia with dispassionate eyes. In that instant he got the impression that she wouldn't care if he killed her. The beast raged to go through the woman to get to Daemon, but the man refused to sacrifice what little honor he had left.

Akia shifted directions just slightly at the last minute, his claws slashing so close to her face that he swore he could feel the cool silk of her skin. He buried his claws into the stone floor. She didn't even flinch.

Daemon shoved the woman forward as he stepped through the cell door slamming it shut.

"Treat his wounds and you may live through the night. Or better yet, sing what I tell you to sing and you can leave right now," Daemon growled through the cell door.

The woman stood there still as a statue, refusing to acknowledge that Daemon even existed. Even lost in his beast, Akia could see she was beautiful. She was tiny and delicate. Her skin had a golden glow to it framed by her long waterfall of black hair. She looked regal even in her simple tunic dress with its wide sleeves. But it was her eyes that captured your attention. Her eyes sparkled like the rarest of cut gems. They were amethyst in color with a flash of golden fire when she turned her eyes on you. It gave the impression that they almost glowed. Even among the jewel-like eyes of the native women that had been thrust in his cell, he had never seen eyes like hers.

Daemon was taking a chance that Akia's honor and sanity would hold in order to intimidate this girl. Akia could see that he had hoped that facing the snarling beast would be enough to get her to cooperate. Daemon turned and stalked off with a roar. The man would never not follow through with a threat, even if it cost him money, because that would be seen as a sign of weakness. So for better or worse it looked like Akia had a cellmate for the night.

CHAPTER TWO

Akia prowled around the woman on all fours. The beast was strong and his siren hadn't began singing yet. If she didn't sing tonight he wondered if he would be trapped as the beast forever. He growled at her; the woman stood there stoically. He charged and retreated but she didn't flinch. It made the man inside the beast curious about what Daemon had inflicted upon her when she seemed unfazed by the most feared monster.

He acted like a feral and afraid animal around her. Approaching only to retreat. When she finally decided to sit down cross legged he had jumped away. The unexpected movement had him afraid that she would strike him and his beast would attack. He had no wish to harm her.

But she just sat there quietly in a meditative pose. Her strange jeweled eyes closed, her breathing even, and her body relaxed. She had a peace about her that radiated into the rest of the room.

Akia's pacing slowed. He studied the woman as he circled her. She was older than he had first thought. On Vukasin her stature would be that of a young child. But he knew through his interactions with the Earth women that not all species were as large as those on Vukas. He wondered if she was the average of her people, or if she would be considered delicate even among them. That thought alone surprised him. Nothing had peaked his curiosity since arriving in this place. He fought and killed. He plotted and despaired. He didn't think about others; he didn't want to know them because at some point he would probably have to kill them.

But he wanted to know her. It was almost a compulsion. Somehow her peace was pulling him in. His beast circled closer. This had to be a test or a trap. There was no reason for Daemon to upset the routine of Akia's life like this. It was a routine he had created for Akia. Why change it now?

The beast snarled and batted at the air near the woman with his deadly claws. He was careful not to injure her, but he made it known that he didn't trust her. He backed away and resumed his prowling.

The woman didn't react to the implied threat. She sat there in silence meditating. She acted as if she was alone in this cell. Akia didn't know whether to be thankful or angry that she was able to disregard him so easily.

Akia went back to studying the woman. Her hair fascinated him. It was as black as a starless night. There wasn't a single wave or curl. It fell like dark water about her back and shoulders. The length was amazingly long. It pooled on the ground around her as she sat on the cell floor. He didn't know of any woman who had such long hair.

Unconsciously he moved closer and closer to her. He circled around behind her and drew in her scent. She smelled like he thought paradise must. It was a pure, fresh scent with a hint of tropical flowers and spice. It was a scent that he knew he would be able to track anywhere. He would always be able to find his woman.

She was his. The thought slammed into his mind. The beast had decided. She would be their mate. The man knew that was an instinctual thought. He also knew it wouldn't be fair to burden any woman, let alone this exquisite creature, with one such as he. So he made a concession to the beast.

The man within added her safety and freedom to his list of unfinished business. He would die before leaving her behind. Daemon didn't realize what he had done, but putting this woman in Akia's path made the beast even more deadly.

The beast circled around to the front of the woman. Its hot breath made her hair flutter across her skin. It stayed there watching her with an unblinking gaze. Part of the beast wanted to turn and retreat. The woman was dangerous in a way that nothing else in this place was; however, he had decided she was theirs. The need to possess warred with the need for safety. In the end possession won and the beast remained at her side.

He, the great and feared monster, flinched when she raised her hand without even opening her eyes. Even without the aid of her eyes, she seemed to know exactly where Akia was. While he knew that she couldn't physically harm him, somehow he knew that if she touched him it would change his world forever. Her delicate hand sank into the fur covering his shoulder, not giving him a chance to move away. She tenderly stroked him, like one might a beloved pet.

Akia didn't care if she saw him as a pet. He whined, all of the pain and despair rushing to the surface of his mind in contrast to her gentle touch. The feel of her soft touch when all he had felt for the past year were beatings and pain was heaven. He couldn't stop the beast from leaning into her touch, begging for more.

She obliged him by bringing her other hand up as well. She scratched and stroked him until he laid down. His head was cradled in her lap. Akia looked up at her while she watched him with her piercing jeweled eyes. As they gazed at each other a connection seemed to build a bridge between them. Something in her gaze calmed the beast's heart; and he closed his eyes to rest, even if it was only for a little while.

She continued to pet him as his nervous panting was replaced with even breathing. His body relaxed. Though he remained the beast because his mystical siren never sang that night. But it didn't seem to matter. Even as the beast, he had found a measure of peace at the touch of the strange woman. He would protect her, even if it was simply as her pet. He had the thought that he could be quite happy as her pet.

His eyes closed. He was so very tired. Tired of fighting for no reason. Tired of hurting. Tired of being alone.

As he drifted off into slumber, the first quiet notes floated through the air. The language was strange and unfamiliar, but he recognized that voice. He would know it anywhere. The music fluttered over his skin and sank into his mind. She had found him. His siren.

CHAPTER THREE

Zamira hadn't felt true fear until that day. She had tried to explain to Daemon of the Tanis that she couldn't just sing anything. She had to sing the songs that the goddess put into her heart. Of course that wasn't quite entirely true. If she concentrated hard enough she could use the power of her voice at any time; it was just easier when acting on instinct. This had angered the man, who wanted her to use her gift to increase his profits, not cause his patrons to burst into tears. It seems that some of the wealthiest visitors to the "new and improved" Ludus Prime found the emotional catharsis uncomfortable and were threatening not to come back. He had changed her world from a peaceful civilization to a den of iniquity; but he couldn't change her

Zamira knew that they would return. Her songs could be addictive. She wasn't prideful, but she knew that what she was able to do with her voice was a unique gift from the goddess. Her eyes had given her away as a child and she had been sent to the temple complex so her gift could be nurtured and trained. Every siren had the potential to be dangerous. They could mesmerize and influence with their voice. This was the reason why anyone with a siren's eyes was sent to the temple, so they could be taught control and given a moral compass. It made for a lonely childhood away from family and without friends. But she understood the necessity of it.

Even as a child the power of her gift frightened and awed the priestesses. Zamira was a thing of legend. Usually there were only a handful of sirens in a generation. Most sirens could evoke emotion and influence thought for a single individual at a time, maybe a handful if they were extremely talented. Zamira could mesmerize entire villages. Anyone who heard her voice felt the need to stop and listen. Only one other voice even came close to Zamira's and that was Lali's. The girls had grown up in the temple together. They were often shunned and feared because of their strong gift, so the two girls spent much of their time together. It had been a long time since Zamira had thought of Lali.

The priestesses trained them to use their gift to help guide pilgrims to the answers they were seeking. Part of that training was recognizing the song that the goddess gave them. For this reason, Zamira refused to sing songs designed to make the patrons to Daemon's fights and casinos reckless and jovial. In her heart she knew that those people who frequented his establishment did so because they were refusing to acknowledge that something was missing in their soul.

Daemon tried to intimidate her by threatening to put her in with the fighter known as the Vukasin Beast. She had been forced to watch some of the gladiatorial matches as a decoration on Daemon's arm. She had seen the fierce brutality of the Beast; but she also saw something deeper. It was for him that she had sung these last few nights. Songs so heart breaking that even Daemon had been forced to tears. This was how she found herself at the Beast's cell.

She heard the battle raging with the guards long before Daemon had dragged her to the cell door. Zamira watched as the Beast dispatched the last guard. His cell was empty except for the bodies of those sent to tame him. He wasn't even afforded the basic comfort of a pallet or blanket like the other fighters. It made her heart break for him. Even she acknowledged that her sympathy was odd considering the brutality of the creature before her; but the goddess had laid a connection to this violent beast in Zamira's heart, only time would tell why.

The beast turned and smiled maliciously at Daemon before it charged. It had raised its claws for a killing blow when Daemon pulled her roughly in front of him. It took all of her training not to react to the pain Daemon caused with his bruising grip on her arm; somehow she knew that would just enrage the beast further.

The beast could have shredded through her to kill Daemon, a desire that blazed in his furious eyes. But at the last second, he shifted the descent of his claws to barely miss her. She could feel the brush of his fur along her cheek. He buried those claws in the ground at her feet with a crushing force. When he prowled away, Zamira took a chance to glance at the gouges in the stone. He hadn't just scratched the surface, holes that were inches deep were at the epicenter of cracked stone. The force and strength needed to do such a thing was astonishing...

Daemon took advantage of the beast's retreat to shove her forward and run from the cell. She would have fallen if not for her natural grace. She stumbled but quickly stood upright and composed again. One last time he demanded she sing the songs he chose. She ignored him. She would rather take her chances with the beast than go against her goddess.

Zamira closed her eyes and meditated on how her path led her to this place. She could feel the beast circling her, but she pushed him from her mind. He would kill or he would not. Nothing would change that so why expend the energy to worry about it?

When Zamira had been a girl on the brink of becoming a woman her world was peaceful and ordered, even if it was lonely. Ludus Prime was a matriarchal society since the dawn of memory. It wasn't a requirement, but because the queens tended to favor long hair, the length of a woman's hair was often seen as a sign of their status. Even in these dark times, Zamira had difficulty with the idea of cutting her hair. It felt like she would be giving up her status as the high priestess.

Because of the matriarchal nature of their society, daughters were so favored that after countless generations males had become scarce. It was a biological necessity that a woman needed a male to continue her line and in recent generations males capitalized on their scarcity. They were able to amass vast fortunes and live like kings among the village women.

Then the Tanis appeared. At first the woman thought that they had been a gift from the goddess for they were tall handsome warriors, worthy of fathering strong daughters. But it quickly became apparent that they did not hold the feminine sacred like the Ludusites did. Zamira often wondered if the Tanis were a trial from the goddess to show the women of Ludus Prime that their arrogance was not the correct path. It would be the goddess's justice that the proud women were now treated like a commodity much in the same fashion that they had treated the males of their planet.

All of this led her mind back to the creature she was now locked away with. She had faith that the goddess would protect her. Despite the fierce posturing, Zamira was confident that the beast didn't want to hurt her. If it was as unfeeling and deadly as its reputation it would have killed her to get to Daemon. Now there was a man she would gladly see dead. That was a decidedly un-priestess like thought. She was supposed to value all life; however, her recent experiences had taught her that some lives are better destroyed for the greater good. Daemon Tanis was one such life.

She could feel the beast just inches from her face. Its breath was warm against her skin. For better or worse, she took a chance and reached up to touch the creature. She felt him flinch when her fingers sank into his fur, but he didn't retreat. His fur was warm and much softer than she would have imagined.

She opened her eyes and watched as her touch melted the tension from the enormous creature. He practically crawled into her lap trying to soak up as much affection as possible. Zamira wondered what his life was like before Daemon because something told her that even before his imprisonment here there was little affection in his life.

He laid his head down across her legs. He was finally relaxed. His breathing wasn't stressed panting, rather it was deep and even. He looked up into her eyes as she watched him. She gazed deep and was surprised to feel the pull of her goddess. Somehow this creature was a part of her destiny.

She felt the need to sing an ancient lullaby as he closed his eyes. The tones were soft and low, the melody sweet. She felt him drift off into sleep as she sang. Then something extraordinary happened. The beast slowly disappeared.

Zamira knew that some of the Tanis males could shift from man to beast, but the creatures thrown into the fighting pits had always remained vicious furred beasts, stuck in those monstrous forms because of the experiments of the Tanis. She had assumed that this creature was one stuck in the body of the beast. It was a lesson from the goddess not to assume.

By the time her song had ended, the man was sound asleep. Zamira studied him. He was a handsome one. He was muscular with a strong jaw. She could tell his skin was naturally a shade or two darker than her own, though it carried the greyish cast of someone who had not seen the sun for many months. The fur had retreated from his body, but his head carried a pelt of thick dark hair. It wasn't the black she was used to seeing among her people. It was dark brown like the richest soil and held hints of other colors. Scars covered his back in testament to the brutal treatment the gladiators endured and battles he had won.

Zamira picked up one of his callused hands. She had seen him kill. He was deadly and dangerous. But he didn't kill indiscriminately. She had heard the stories of the other women sent into his cell. He had terrified them, yet they came out without a single injury while the guards, who were easily twice the size and strength of the women, regularly died when they entered his cell. That told Zamira that he chose not to harm the women.

Somewhere under the broken beast was an honorable man.

Zamira carefully shifted his head from her lap and she laid down next to him. It had been a long, stressful day and she was exhausted. In his sleep the man sought Zamira's warmth and touch. She smiled a bit as she wrapped an arm around his waist and cuddled his back. He dwarfed her, so she was completely hidden from the door as even in his sleep he shifted to place himself between her and possible danger. His bulk also had the added bonus of blocking from her sight the bodies of the dead guards Daemon had just left in the cell.

Zamira shuttered at the thought of being surrounding by death. Death was becoming such a regular part of Zamira's life that she no longer cried at a senseless loss of life. She was learning that a certain amount of emotional distance was necessary for survival.

With his strong, scarred back the only thing in her vision, Zamira fell asleep next to her beast of a man.

CHAPTER FOUR

Akia awoke to the feeling of a small warm body pressed against his back. He ran his hand through his shaggy hair and stopped and stared at it. He was a man again. He was fairly certain that he had gone to sleep as the beast. Then it came back to him.

He rolled over and studied the sleeping face of his siren. She was as beautiful as her voice. He couldn't resist the urge to gently push her hair away from her delicate face. She seemed so fragile but he knew that to be an illusion. She had stood and faced the monster everyone feared with peaceful composure. He knew there was a will of iron under her delicate features.

Her eyes fluttered open at his touch. Akia felt like he could fall into their depths.

"Good morning," Akia's voice sounded rough from disuse even to his own ears.

The woman's smile was gentle and mysterious. It left the impression that she knew the wonders of the universe. When she didn't answer immediately he wondered if she had received the translation implant. He could have sworn Daemon had spoken to her in Vukasin, but his memories while in the body of the beast could be hazy.

She laughed, a sound that echoed through his heart like the sun driving away the darkness.

"I understand you perfectly well, warrior."

Akia look to see if he had given her the mating bite in his beast like state. He frowned in confusion when he discovered there was no reason for her to be able to read his thoughts.

She smiled and patted his cheek. "I did not read your mind. Your questions were obvious."

"I did not harm you last night."

"Of course not. I knew you wouldn't before they dragged me to this place. You are an honorable warrior."

"I am a killing beast," Akia spat and rolled away from her. He roughly gathered up the bodies from the night before and stacked them near the cell door.

"There is no dishonor in killing your enemies." The woman stood up and placed a hand on his bicep. "I hear the stories; I have seen the evidence with my own eyes. You kill your enemies but you do not willfully harm the innocent." She sat down and gestured for him to sit next to her, "Come…I must treat your wounds before Daemon returns."

"I will not take the strength enhancing drugs," Akia growled as he sat down.

"No drugs, just a salve to speed the healing and a portable regen unit to close any open wounds."

She pulled the small pack that had been slung across her torso in front of her. With a nod from Akia she began treating his wounds from last night's battle.

"What are you called?"

"A gentleman would offer his name first before asking for a woman's." Her tone was light so he knew that she was teasing him.

"I am sure you have heard that I am the Vukasin Beast."

"That may be what they call you, but that is not who you are. I want to know what you call yourself."

"Akia…I am Akia of the Clan Tiaret."

"Zamira."

*****

'Zamira…the name was as beautiful as she was,' Akia thought.

The beast in him practically purred at her gentle touch. He sighed when she took her hands away to grab the regeneration unit. She ran it over his skin in a way that told him she had some practice with the device. The paranoid part of him wondered how she learned to use the Vukasin device. In the light of day with more of the man's logic rather than the beast's reaction he had to acknowledge that this could still be an elaborate ruse created by Daemon.

The beast in him roared that he didn't care. Zamira was his. It didn't matter why she was here. His muscles tensed as he battled to keep control. Being around the woman had him off balance.

Zamira hummed a soothing tune and the tension melted from Akia's body. Her ability to sooth the savage beast within could be a dangerous thing if she turned out to be an enemy. Akia reached up and stopped her ministrations. He kept a hold of her hand and pulled her in front of him.

He studied her with an unblinking gaze. At first glance she seemed fragile and innocent. Her large eyes called at something protective deep within him. But he remembered flashes of her facing down his raging beast the night before. There is a quiet strength in her that rivaled most soldiers.

"Who are you?" he asked.

*****

Zamira felt the beast lurking behind Akia's eyes. He was studying her with the eyes of a predator. She shouldn't blame him for his doubt. Goddess knows enemies lurked around every corner. But she was still hurt. She had felt a connection to him last night and she thought he had felt the same when his beast calmed in her presence. Perhaps the goddess's call didn't extend to Vukasins.

For the first time in her life Zamira was unsure of her path. She knew she felt a connection to this man, but she had assumed that he would feel something in return to help guide them on the path the goddess wished for them to take.

She could hear the accusation in his voice when he asked who she was. He didn't trust her.

Logically she knew he had no reason to trust her. So she would have to earn his trust.

"I am Zamira, high priestess to the Goddess of the Hidden Path, Ti'lak."

She shivered as Akia's thumb made small circles on the wrist he hadn't relinquished. It was an unconscious, gentle motion that gave Zamira hope that he might view her one day as something other than a threat.

"What does that mean?"

Zamira wasn't sure how to answer him. But before she could launch into an explanation of her world's customs and culture, Akia whipped away from her and started growling low in his throat. She watched in fascination as dark fur rippled across his skin, appearing and disappearing in waves. His agitation was obvious. Zamira was about to ask what was wrong when she finally heard a sound: booted footsteps outside of the cell door.

Akia shoved Zamira behind his back. She tried to peek over his shoulder but was too short. She had to look around his torso and saw Daemon with a squad of soldiers enter the cell. Akia lost all control of his beast when Daemon entered his territory. The transformation was much quicker than his change last night. Zamira blinked and instead of the man a dark growling beast shielded her.

Daemon eyed the snarling beast before him. "I see the little lady was able to accomplish something no one else has been able to." He gave Akia an evil smirk. "I'll remember to send her in to treat you next time your opponent gets the best of you. Now if you would be so kind as to hand her over, I have use for her."

Akia kept his body between Zamira and Daemon's men. He wasn't going to let her go without a fight. She watched as he bared his fangs and snapped at the terrified soldiers. Everyone knew of the beast's reputation. Those men knew that there was a good chance they wouldn't make it out alive from this assignment. Not that Daemon cared that he was possibly throwing away his soldiers' lives. There always seemed to be more to replace those lost.

With a wave of Daemon's hand more soldiers spilled into the crowded cell. The front line of soldiers knelt with energy shields, while a second line stood behind them. Akia's claws and teeth kept most at arm's length. Zamira knew that if she hadn't been there Akia would have already engaged his enemy in battle; but he refused to leave her unprotected and that became his handicap.

"Now!" Daemon shouted the order and the second line raised an archaic weapon that Zamira was all too familiar with. She tried to push her way in front of Akia before the soldiers fired the blow guns. She had no way of knowing which of the many poisons her planet was familiar with laced the tips of the darts. Some could incapacitate while others brought a swift death.

Akia blocked her attempts to protect him. Zamira screamed when she heard the darts impact his body. She counted at least half a dozen. In such a large dose even the tranquilizers and paralytics could be fatal.

Daemon grabbed her arm as she tried to catch Akia's falling body. He dragged her away. She dug in her heels and scratched and fought, but his much larger bulk and strength made it impossible to get away.

"Don't worry, I'm not going to kill my credit maker just yet." Daemon laughed, "He's got a few more fights left in him."

Zamira kept her eyes on Akia until they shut his cell door and sealed him away from her sight.

CHAPTER FIVE

Akia woke with his head pounding. He raised a hand to massage his temple only to have it stop short of his head. He pulled on one arm and then the other, both restricted in movement. His momentary confusion gave way to rage and panic. That *frexing* son of a buzzard-raptor had him chained.

Akia franticly scanned the room. This was not his normal cell. The walls were metallic and he could see monitoring equipment to his left side. His eyes narrowed on Daemon's massive form; he was sitting in a chair across the room, sipping on a glass of wine.

"If you are looking for the pretty little songstress, she's not here." Daemon uncrossed his legs and leaned forward. "I'm really quite disappointed. I fully expected the Vukasin Beast to scare the dragon-spider shit out of her. But it seems that she was able to tame the savage beast."

With a powerful thrust of his legs, Akia strained against his bonds. Phasing as he pushed his muscles to their limit. Daemon signaled to someone at the door, completely ignoring the thrashing beast in the floor in front of him.

"You should feel honored. I had those chains specially constructed just for you. One good thing about this backwater planet is the discovery of a new alloy. The scientists are still debating what to call it. But it doesn't matter, they are almost impossible to break."

Akia growled at Daemon. His gaze suddenly shifted focus as several men in lab uniforms spilled into the cell followed by a squad of soldiers.

"Muzzle him first, otherwise he will tear you apart even chained." Daemon stood and knocked back the last of his wine. "He's missed a half dozen doses and I have a particularly brutal opponent planned in the next few nights. Dose him as high as you can."

"At those levels he could go rabid," said a lab assistant.

Daemon grabbed the insolent man by his throat and dangled him in the air. "I would suggest you be careful with your dosing then. Take him to the edge but not over or you will take his place in the arena." He threw the man down and stalked out of the cell.

Soldiers in tight formation marched toward Akia. He snarled and snapped, saliva dripping from his sharp fangs. The men sent to subdue him were getting smarter. They overlapped their pulse shields and used the field to pin the beast to the ground.

When he was immobile only one soldier eased his shield away from Akia's biting jaws, but he didn't lift it enough to allow Akia to move his head. Another soldier wrestled a mesh muzzle made of the same metal that chained him to the floor onto Akia's jaws.

Before the soldier could complete the task, Akia was able to bite down on his hand. He grinned a feral grin when he heard bones crunch. But that had been anticipated since another soldier smoothly stepped in to complete the job while the beast was distracted.

It was an almost comical sight: a dozen soldiers dog piled on top of a trussed gladiator slave. Even then the pile of men was having a difficult time subduing a single beast. The lab technicians would approach with injector in hand only to back off when Akia bucked, lifting the soldiers off the ground.

"Let's wait until he exhausts himself before administering the drug," the lab assistant who challenged Daemon croaked out through his injured throat.

"Have you seen this thing in the arena?" the injured soldier said shaking his head. "He doesn't get tired. That is how he defeats a lot of his challengers, he out lasts them."

Akia bucked again nearly dislodging the soldiers pressing his shoulders to the floor.

"Get your ass over here and inject him! We aren't going to be able to control him for much longer."

There was a brief game of 'no, you do it' as the injector was passed around the various technicians. Finally, the senior lab technician pulled rank and ordered the lowly assistant to do it.

"Are you sure about this dose?"

"As sure as we can be. I did err slightly on the side of caution but it should be a high enough dose to satisfy Lord Daemon."

"What about the subject going rabid?"

The senior lab tech shrugged. "There are never any guarantees, but considering the subject's high tolerance for previous administrations I think we are safe." He handed the assistant a second injector. "This should knock him out and give the drug enough time to assimilate if you are worried about it. Just make sure you inject the other one first as we need the rapid heartbeat to disperse the drug to all systems quickly."

The nervous lab assistant approached the growling beast on the floor. The soldier closest to him barked an order to get it done when he looked like he was about to baulk. Another solder lifted his pulse shield from the beast's shoulder but made sure to keep the claw pinned. As fast as the lab assistant could manage in his fumbling, he stabbed the injector with the enhancing drug into Akia's shoulder. Akia howled in frustration which almost made the assistant drop the sedative. He recovered and quickly injected the second vial into Akia.

The soldiers kept Akia pinned until his movements became uncoordinated. When the mission was accomplished, the lab techs and soldiers carefully backed away from the sluggish claws of the enraged beast. They stayed against the far wall until the creature collapsed. The senior lab technician checked Akia's vitals. Once assured that he was alive but unconscious, the soldiers and techs left the cell. They disregarded the poor creature who had reverted back to a man chained to the floor.

CHAPTER SIX

Zamira picked at the stone wall of her cell, using her finger nails to scratch images into the surface. She was locked away, alone and in darkness, once more. It had been weeks since she had any real contact with Akia, not since Daemon had dragged her away that day from Akia's cell and locked her into her own tiny cell. He was furious that her night with "The Beast" didn't scare her into compliance. Still he forced her to sing.

That first night she had sung a heartbreaking melody while Akia's rage could be heard over the din of the casino. But she didn't sing for the masses. She sang for one tortured soul. Her dark melody and the unearthly howls of Akia wove together to create the miasma of a haunted atmosphere even among the bright lights of the casino. It left the audience speculating if Daemon's resort was cursed.

Zamira smiled. It amazed her how even technologically advanced species could still be so superstitious. She hoped the goddess had cursed Daemon. What him and those like him were doing to not only her people but their own deserved punishment.

Part of her wanted to be the one to have a hand in that retribution. Yet whenever she tried to think it through or make plans, her mind wandered back to the one creature that everyone on this planet was afraid of - everyone except her.

Zamira wasn't arrogant enough to overlook the signs the goddess had put in her path. Even her own heart and mind told her that her path wasn't one of revenge, but that of healing. Akia needed her. Now more than ever. She had heard the rumors. Daemon was experimenting on his gladiators, especially Akia.

She turned and leaned against the stone wall and sighed. Daemon had forced her to watch some of Akia's battles. Something had changed in him after she had been taken away. She was fairly certain that Daemon and his minions were responsible for this.

Akia was more brutal and fierce than ever. Before he said he could walk in as the man and shift during the battle at a strategic moment. Now she watched him as he entered fully phased, all claws, teeth and fur. He would raise his elongated snout to the air when he walked into the arena as the Vukasin Beast, searching for something. Then his eyes would lock on her and he would explode in rage and violence. He killed off his enemies quickly and would stare at her as he backed out of the arena.

Daemon raged when he killed a high credit opponent last night in under a minute. Evidently the patrons wanted more of a show. Not to mention his profits on the betting had seriously dropped. Word had spread that no matter the odds, never bet against the Beast.

Zamira jumped when a howl of rage echoed through building. Evidently, Akia had discovered that Daemon had not brought her to this fight. He was trying to test a theory that perhaps there would be more of a show in her absence. She could have told him that it wouldn't make a difference. Akia wasn't the kind of man to be dictated to.

She settled back against the stone and thought about the man who filled her thoughts and dreams here lately. She had been drawn to him when he had been just another gladiator slave; trying to catch glimpses of him as he passed on his way to the arena. Even in his furry form she looked for him. She hadn't known at the time that the beast was also a man. Even if she had never found out he still caught her attention in both forms.

She had been enthralled those times Daemon had her escort him to the matches and Akia was fighting. His body moved like he was dancing even in battle. In the past she was drawn to both the beast and the man separately, now she can't get the whole person out of her thoughts. She had felt so many new songs swell up into her heart. She hadn't sung them yet. Those songs were meant for only one person and she had spent only one innocent night with him.

She was so distracted by her thoughts that she hadn't heard Daemon's approach until he flung the cell door open, blinding her with bright lights invading her darkness.

"Get up," he huffed.

Zamira pushed off the ground and stood, making no move to close the distance between her and Daemon.

Daemon stepped into her cell and grabbed her arm in a bruising grip, dragging her out of the darkness.

"I watched the surveillance recording of the night you and the beast were housed together. I don't know what magic you weaved then but you will calm him now or I will kill you both!"

Daemon didn't drag her to the gladiator cells like before. Instead he took her back towards the arena.

Sounds of battle and the agonized cries of men dying filled the halls. As they neared the entrance to the arena, Zamira could hear the spectators' screams. Daemon shoved her over the threshold into the arena.

Zamira gasped and blinked away the tears in her eyes. She had become familiar with death since the Tanis had come to Ludus Prime, but carnage on this scale was something she was entirely unfamiliar with.

She took a step forward trying to find Akia in the fray. She shivered when her bare foot stepped in something warm, wet, and sticky. She dared not look down for fear of losing her composure.

Zamira stopped to take a calming breath when she felt a sharp hit on her back, nearly causing her to fall over. She looked over her shoulder to see a scowling Daemon with an ornamental blade drawn. He used the knife to indicate that she should continue walking. Zamira squared her shoulders and walked on.

She surveyed the area around her. Patrons were climbing over themselves to escape as soldiers tried to climb the arena walls to get away from the death that stalked them. Zamira skirted around the shredded bodies of several ludaks - giant hulking beasts from her planet's deepest swamps. They were vicious creatures and even the most experienced warriors hesitated when confronting them. But Akia had killed several with ease.

Daemon had evidently decided that dumb animals acting on instinct were no match for the raging Vukasin Beast. The bodies of the ludaks gave way to nearly unrecognizable mounds of flesh. Zamira wouldn't have known they were once men if the occasional arm, weapon, and armor weren't laying in the middle of the mangled flesh.

Then she saw him...her beast. Daemon's minions were no longer trying to contain him. They were trying to kill him. But Akia made that goal nearly impossible. Daemon had made a tactical error when he used drugs to increase Akia's savagery and strength. He created a monster that he could no longer control.

Zamira covered her mouth, willing the scream climbing up her throat to retreat. Her vision blurred with unshed tears. How could they do this to an honorable man? She knew that these senseless deaths would weigh heavily on Akia's soul. But even she could see he had no choice. Daemon had created a kill or be killed scenario.

She felt a sharp point in her back. Daemon

shoved her forward with the point of his blade. Zamira could feel a trickle of blood drip down her back. She ignored it and stepped forward away from his blade.

"Calm him or I slice your throat right here," Daemon threatened.

"I'm not sure I can." Zamira sighed and turned to face Daemon. There was no fear in her eyes. That look always pissed him off because it reminded him of another woman who faced him without fear. That woman, Megan, was the source of his greatest humiliation when she defeated him in a challenge battle right before the *Mate Avi Keiger.*

"You better hope you can or you won't walk away from this arena alive."

Zamira shrugged and turned away from Daemon's growled threat. She would try but not because she feared death. She knew that even in his rampage Akia would try to protect her as soon as he realized she was there. She had faith in the connection her goddess showed her. No, she would try because if Akia didn't calm soon he would be lost forever. Whether that loss came because the Tanis finally killed him or he lost his soul to the beast didn't matter; he would be lost either way.

Zamira drew herself up to her full diminutive height. She took a deep breath and centered her spirit. Before she could sing Akia's song she had to get his attention. But if she wasn't careful his enemies would use his distraction to destroy him. She had to call upon her greatest gift and enthrall everyone within the sound of her voice. This was a trick that she hadn't used since she was an adolescent in training at the temple. It was the one and only time that her trainer had actually struck her. It had been drilled into her to never reveal the full scope of her abilities unless it was a dire emergency. To her saving Akia was just such an emergency.

She released a single pure tone and projected it to the furthest corners of the arena. The din of battle fell into silence. Soldiers, patrons, and beasts all froze under the power of her voice. Even Daemon gazed at her in awe, unable to move. Everyone stopped until the only thing that existed was a single note that held the power of the universe's creation within it.

When everyone was held within her power Zamira began to sing. It was a song the goddess had laid in her heart that night she stayed with Akia. She had been afraid to sing it then because of the meaning it held within. It was a song that offered both solace and destruction. With it she would offer herself to Akia. It was a song filled with hope and unconditional love. Man or beast, this song spoke of choosing him and only him.

Zamira was terrified of what that song meant for both her and Akia; nevertheless, it swelled within her and she knew in her heart of hearts she had to sing it now or she would lose her honorable warrior forever.

CHAPTER SEVEN

Akia's claws froze midair. He was inches away from gutting yet another enemy when the mystical sound pierced his mind and soul. His siren had come at last. Somewhere in his animal brain he knew that his rage had been caused by her absence. The beast wanted to be angry with her for abandoning him. However, what little of the man remained rationalized that she hadn't left him by choice.

Everything faded away except for that single

note. His enemies no longer mattered. His rage no longer mattered. She was the only thing that mattered.

Then she started to sing. Zamira…her name and voice were a beacon calling him back from the abyss. She told him that she needed him in her song. The notes spoke that she wanted him. Love that could either save him or destroy him was being offered within the notes that filtered through the air to land in his psyche.

Akia was almost afraid to hope. Was the message he was receiving the truth or a creation of his fevered brain? He threw aside the soldier he held in his grip and in his beast form he turned to the source of the music that had them all captivated.

His feverish predator's eyes found her sparkling jeweled ones. His gaze searched hers and he found…acceptance and love. Beast or man, his soul knew this woman was made for him and he would find a way for them to be together and may the gods have mercy on anyone who stood in the way.

Akia was the only one able to move within her song because it was his song. She had given it to him with an open heart and he now owned it. He walked away from the carnage, his body slowly shifting with each step, until he stood before her a man once more.

She gazed into his eyes, unshed tears shimmering

in her own eyes. He recognized that she had been afraid that he might reject her beloved gift of love. But he was not so far gone as to not recognize it for the miracle and blessing that it was.

As the last note echoed between them, he reached out to take hold of his woman. She moved to go to him but was jerked backed with a painful cry.

The beast fought to emerge at the sight of Daemon holding a knife to his mate's throat. Akia growled as the blade pricked her skin. Daemon didn't know it but he had signed his death warrant, sooner rather than later, with the small trickle of blood that trailed down her throat.

"Back, beast, or the woman dies." Daemon jerked Zamira to him. She couldn't help the cry of pain that escaped as he wrenched her arm behind her back to control her movements.

Fangs burst forth in Akia's mouth and fur rippled across his body as he let lose a feral growl.

"Keep control of your beast if you want her to live."

Akia struggled to retain control. He knew that Daemon would follow through on his threat and despite the knowledge that Daemon wouldn't leave the arena alive if he harmed Zamira, Akia wasn't willing to risk her death.

Daemon smiled as the beast settled, convinced that he now had the upper hand. He pulled Zamira close and with an evil smirk licked her cheek. She struggled to get away which just caused the knife at her throat to cut her deeper.

Akia advanced toward the pair with a growl.

"Tsk, tsk…you get within striking distance of me and I slit her throat." Daemon chuckled and glared at Akia. "What do you think the songbird's last sound would be?"

Akia stopped his advance but the deep growl echoed through the now silent arena. The patrons who hadn't been able to flee watched with rapt attention. Akia knew that his enemy was playing to the audience.

"What do you want, Daemon?"

Daemon pulled the knife away from Zamira's throat and gave a flourishing bow, but he didn't ease his grip on the arm behind her back. "I want what I have always wanted." He raised his blade to the stands and continued, "To give these good people the most entertaining show."

"Let her go, Daemon," Akia hissed through clenched teeth.

The Tanis tyrant tapped the point of his blade to his chin. "I think not. This little beauty is my insurance for your proper behavior. You have been a rather troublesome slave. I might not be able to break you, but can you say the same about her?" Daemon wrenched Zamira's arm upward until it popped and she screamed.

Fangs burst forth from Akia's jaw and his fist dripped blood where his claws cut into his own skin; but he dared not move while Zamira was in Daemon's grasp. His beast was demanding he attack the threat to its mate but the man knew that without a plan of action attacking now would just get both of them killed. He didn't mind the idea of his own death, but he could not stand the thought of Zamira being taken from this world.

Daemon watched the shifting beast with wary eyes. He signaled his soldiers who quickly scurried to chain Akia. When the men had him secured, Daemon turned and dragged Zamira out of the arena.

The procession marched passed the gladiator cells. The various creatures howled and beat at their metal doors as they neared. Daemon yelled for quiet but the masses ignored him. He had to side step one of the deformed phased that was supposed to have been sent to the arena for a match. The creature had been forgotten when Akia lost control. The deformed lunged and snapped as Daemon and his soldiers walked by; but the creature shrank into a corner and whimpered at Akia's growl and glare when his claws came too close to striking Zamira. Animals always recognized dominance and power.

Daemon jerked Zamira almost off balance and increased his pace. Soon they found themselves in the darkest reaches of the gladiator cells. Zamira had only been here one other time, the night she met Akia face to face.

Daemon stood to the side of the door, Zamira in front of him with the knife back at her throat. The soldiers used stun sticks to push the chained Akia forward into the cell. He barely registered their sting, but moved forward for Zamira's sake. Once in the cell Akia turned and glared silently at Daemon, fur rippling across his face.

Daemon swallowed and started to back away. He saw his death in the beast's eyes. His fist clenched around the hilt of the blade he still held to Zamira's throat. He frowned, and then with a growl, he shoved the dainty woman into Akia's cell and slammed the door shut.

"Keep him calm or I will torture him while you watch," Daemon sneered at Zamira through the tiny window of the cell door.

He may have no power over the male, but he could still intimidate the female. Women were always the weak link when you threatened someone they cared for.

"You will sing the song I tell you to tomorrow night or I will kill him." He turned his scowl on Akia. "You will fight when and where I tell you without pulling stunts like you did tonight. If you don't I will take it out on the female." He turned to leave and with a wave of his hand the guards fell in line behind him.

Akia turned and saw that Zamia cradled her injured arm with her other hand.

"I'm so sorry..." Tears welled up into Akia's eyes and he bowed his head. He felt useless. He couldn't even protect those that were dear to him.

"Shhh," Zamira rushed to him and cupped his cheek with her good hand. "As long as we are together we will find a way." She lifted his chin until his eyes focused on hers. She smiled a mischievous smile that seemed so out of place in their dire circumstances. "Besides, I'm not without my own hidden talents."

She pulled a small crystal control pad out of her dress sleeve. At the question in Akia's eyes Zamira shrugged. "It was a skill one of the street girls I used to sneak out and play with taught me when I was a child at the temple."

She walked behind Akia and laid the control pad on the shackles that bound his wrists together. After pressing a few controls the shackles fell to the stone floor with a metallic clang.

CHAPTER EIGHT

Akia grabbed Zamira in a crushing embrace.

"Argh!"

Akia jumped back at her cry of pain. "Sorry." He raised his hand and caught the tear trailing down her cheek. "I thought I had lost you, *jinaria*. If that ever happens I would have truly become the monster you saw today."

Zamira started to refute his claim but Akia cut her off by gently manipulating her injured arm. She sucked in her breath to keep from screaming out loud, though it echoed through her mind.

"I don't feel any broken bones; but it is definitely dislocated." He looked into Zamira's eyes with a grimace. "I can fix it, but it is going to hurt like the five hells."

She clenched her teeth and closed her eyes tightly with a nod. Akia gently laid her on the ground and lined her arm up next to her body. He braced himself and took a deep breath. With a firm pull he realigned her shoulder with a pop.

Zamira cried out at the sudden excruciating pain, but was surprised when almost as soon as her shoulder popped the pain receded.

Akia took off his tunic shirt and ripped it in half. Zamira couldn't seem to look away as his bared muscles moved during the task. Her insides clenched and heat pooled between her legs. As a priestess on a planet of mostly women she had only seen males without their shirt on when they were sent to her to attempt breeding. And the few she remembered were pale imitations compared to the sculpted beauty of Akia's bare chest and stomach. Never before had a male drawn her interest in such a visceral fashion.

"Huh? Wha...?" Zamira realized that he had been talking to her while she was lost in her ogling.

Akia loomed over her and gently wrapped the remains of his shirt around her arm and tied the ends around her neck, creating a cradling sling.

"I said it would be best to limit the use of your arm for a few days so your shoulder can heal. As much as I don't want to ask anything of the bastard, maybe Daemon will let you use a regen unit to speed the healing."

Zamira reached up with her good hand and traced his scruffy cheek and jaw. She then lifted herself up to place a tentative kiss on his lips. When he didn't pull away, she braved tracing her tongue across his lips. With a growl Akia took the kiss over and she was lost. Zamira felt like she needed to be so close to Akia that she was inside his skin. It was a primal need, a calling from the goddess. She knew that this man was meant to be hers and she his.

She used her good arm to try and frantically pull her dress up her body. She wanted to feel him skin to skin. Her movements seemed to jolt Akia out of their mutual lustful haze and he pulled away, leaving her lips grasping only at air.

He pushed himself up and paced away. "We can't do this."

Zamira awkwardly readjusted her dress with her good arm. She felt cold, not just because his moving away deprived her of the heat of his body but because he rejected her. She had never been rejected before. Of course all the males sent to her knew what was expected. It was merely a means to an end, albeit a pleasurable one in most cases. The men were interchangeable because she had no emotional connection to them or the act. She was beginning to learn that emotions made the act of sex complicated and messy.

She wanted Akia, not just because he was a fine male specimen but because she felt something deep inside for him. She wanted to know him, spend time with him, share things only with him. It was a confusing but exhilarating experience. She had been doubtful of tales of love until that point. Zamira had foolishly thought that if she ever fell in love that man would naturally love her in return. She had been so sure that Akia and she were goddess blessed; yet he didn't seem to feel the same pull that she did. What was she supposed to do if he didn't want her in the same way she wanted him? She turned away from him, her eyes swimming in tears.

"I'm sorry," she sobbed. "I thought..." she hiccupped and stuffed her fist into her mouth. She won't break down. She was a priestess of Ti'lak. She was always in control. Maybe if she kept telling herself that she would believe it. She dashed away the tears that refused to stop.

She felt the heat of Akia's body behind her as his massive, gentle hands turned her face to his.

"Don't ever think that I don't want you, Zamira."

His voice was deep and gruff as if he choked on his own tears. "You are beautiful and I want nothing more than to strip you bare and feast on you until you scream my name. One day I will pleasure you so thoroughly that your body, mind, and soul will know that you belong to me and I to you."

"Then why not now? I want you too."

Akia laid his forehead against hers. "*Jinaria*, my precious little one…I am barely more than the beast the Tanis have made me. Don't tempt me to dishonor you." He hushed her protests with a gentle kiss. "You know the walls have eyes and ears. After the heat of the moment passed you would realize that you had shared something so precious not just with me but with any number of guards. The very thought of one of those bastards seeing you that way has me on the verge of a murderous rage. You deserve so much more than this." He waved a hand around the bare cell.

"I'm afraid that this is all we will have, Akia. I want something beautiful in this horrid place."

Akia picked up Zamira's hand and kissed her fingertips, "My vow to you…I will get us out of here somehow and when I do you are mine." Akia pulled Zamira to him and wrapped her in his strong arms. "Until then, let me hold you." He laid down and placed Zamira's head on his chest like a pillow.

"I can hear your heart beating," she traced the

sharp muscles of his chest.

"It beats only for you. You are my only reason for living."

His fingers combed through her hair. It was a surprisingly soothing gesture. Zamira hadn't had many people who were allowed to touch her in her role as priestess. When they did it was perfunctory, to bathe her or help her dress in the ceremonial robes. Even the sex had been perfunctory. There was no cuddling or even talking really.

Lying there listening to Akia's heartbeat, Zamira realized that she had missed many simple but important things in her life as a priestess. Then the Tanis came and she went from priestess to slave. The touches then became painful and punishing, though she knew she was fortunate. Her voice had been a precious commodity and she was spared most of the brutal treatment for fear of damaging that source of income.

But Akia's touch was something else entirely. It could both inflamed her and soothe her. She knew he had the power to crush her but with her he was unfailingly gentle. He might be a monster to the rest of the universe, a thing to be feared, but to her he will always be the gentle and honorable man that captured her heart.

"Would you sing for me?"

Zamira's soul swelled with a haunting melody of timeless love. As the notes drifted across her lips, she knew Akia was her goddess-given future and they would find the path there together. He would always be the one person she associated with the feeling of love.

CHAPTER NINE

"Is it true, Kavi?" A breathless Banji burst into the *Khalon's* study, interrupting his meeting with his spy master.

Ghaleb sighed. His subjects were forgetting protocol and acting like this was their family home. He placed the blame squarely on the heads of the Earth females who seemed to have taken over. Evidently a feeling of home and family was important to them and most of them didn't put much stock into formalities that most royal courts adhered to with an almost religious zeal. Most days he actually enjoyed the more relaxed atmosphere around the palace; however, he would have to address the matter of protocol with Reijo. They couldn't have random people bursting in when he was meeting with individuals with secret information.

"You forget you place, *kijani*," Ghaleb barked.

Banji straightened to attention immediately. He didn't blubber or make excuses. It was one of the reasons Ghaleb liked the young man. He owned up to his mistakes.

"Pardon my intrusion," Banji bowed to Ghaleb before straightening back to attention. "I overheard Reijo talking and he mentioned that they may have found Akia."

Kavi looked at Ghaleb and at his subtle nod, Kavi gestured to another chair.

"Sit, boy. We are going to be here a while and knowing you, you are going to insist on being a part of this."

Banji crossed to the other side of the royal study and sat facing the two most powerful men of the Vukasin Empire. His body was noticeably tense but he waited patiently for the other men to take the lead in the conversation.

Ghaleb studied one of the twins that had at one

time been one of the best covert operatives he had. Since finding his mate and starting a family with the Earth woman known as Maria, Banji was much more open about showing the emotions that ran so deeply in him. It had ruined him for most operations. Of course that was a moot point since the man had requested to move to a position instructing the warriors instead of working as an operative the day he discovered that Maria was pregnant. She recently gave birth to twins, a boy and a girl. Another reason why they had tried to keep him out of this.

"For the record, I think it would be best if you left this mission to others and remained here with your mate." Ghaleb raised his hand when Banji started to protest. "But I also know that now that you know we have some intelligence on where your brother might be that you will refuse to stay out of it. I wouldn't put it past you and your mate to launch your own rescue operation."

"Maria and I both feel responsible for Akia's imprisonment. He sacrificed himself so we could escape."

"Something I am fairly certain he would do again." Kavi laid a hand on Banji's arm and gave it a squeeze. He had been a brutal teacher, but he still had a fatherly regard for a few of the men he trained. The twins fell into that number.

"I want to make it perfectly clear that while I will consider allowing you on this mission your mate and offspring stay here." Ghaleb crossed his arms and glared at Banji.

"That won't be a problem. Maria is highly protective of our children. Especially since she won't be able to have any more. I should be able to convince her that it would be best if she stayed behind with them."

Ghaleb relaxed a bit and chuckled. "I wish Megan were so easy to manage."

Banji smiled. Everyone in the Tiaret clan was in equal parts terrified of Megan's temper and loved her to pieces. She had the same presence here at the royal palace when she was here as the wielder of the Spear of Authority or her mate was acting as the *kijani-a* of all of the imperial forces. She blew through like a whirlwind and always got her way; but everyone allowed it because they knew how deeply she cared for the people.

"Sire, Megan is a warrior. You will never be able to change that. Maria is by nature a nurturer. She may fight if it is necessary, but given a choice she would rather not. No two women are the same. Even the native Vukasin women have vastly different personalities."

Kavi nodded his head. "Banji is right. Learn from the mistakes of our past, Ghaleb, and it will build a stronger future."

Ghaleb rolled his eyes. "Fine. Can we get back to the matter at hand?"

Both Kavi and Banji knew the casual discussion was over by the tone of Ghaleb's voice. Kavi brought out a crystal tablet and laid it on the desk in front of Ghaleb. He hit a couple of keys and a holographic image projected into the air above the tablet.

It lit up the room with virtual pyrotechnics of every color. The image of a scantily clad alien beauty appeared along with a voice cycling through the most well-known languages of the universe. When Vukasin was presented as an option, Kavi push an illuminated sphere on the tablet and the recording continued in Vukasin only.

"We invite you to come to the Paradise Casino and Resort on the beautiful world of Ludus Prime. Any luxury you can imagine we can provide, discretion is guaranteed." The holoimage of the woman displayed herself suggestively as the background around her changed. Images of beautiful beaches, vibrant gardens, and spa-like retreats appeared. But if you paid enough attention to the flashing backgrounds you also spotted things that appealed to the darker side of people, such as rooms meant for inflicting pain, a multitude of females (as well as a few males) fawning over a single person, and dens for the consumption of various mind altering substances.

Ghaleb reached out and stopped the recording. "By the gods, the Tanis are running a pleasure house on a global scale. I assume that they are using slave labor to do so?"

Kavi nodded. "There is more."

He started the recording up again. After a few more minutes of extoling the vices of the casino and resort a calendar of events came up. The main events seemed to center around gladiator fights which were advertised as fights to the death. One fight in particular caught everyone's attention: the Vukasin Beast versus the Raynark Rampager.

"How old is this?"

"Approximately two months." Kavi shut off the advertisement and pocketed the crystal. "The various wealthy patrons who receive those invitations are instructed to destroy the crystal afterwards. Slavery might not be illegal in every star system, but the senseless brutality is still frowned upon by most developed societies and the Tanis seem to trying to cultivate political alliances as well as amassing an obscene number of credits. I was able to obtain this because the owner found himself deep in debt to the casino, which seems to be hazardous to your health if you have difficulty paying. He found out we were looking for information about Akia and we came to a mutually beneficial agreement."

"And how much did that cost the royal

treasury?" Ghaleb asked.

Kavi shrugged.

"Are you sure Akia is still alive?" Banji rubbed his chest. His heart hurt. He had been happily building a life with Maria while Akia was forced to fight and kill.

"We sent an operative to infiltrate the Tanis operation on Ludus Prime."

Ghaleb leaned forward and glared at his spymaster. "I'm hearing that tone in your voice again, Kavi. I want to know everything you have found out."

Kavi sighed. "It is much worse than we feared. The Tanis haven't just set up their business operations on Ludus Prime, they have conquered the entire planet. According to my sources the Tanis were welcomed at first as Ludus Prime had a shortage of breeding males. But their superior strength and warrior training soon had the peaceful inhabitants under their thumb. They have basically enslaved the entire population and destroyed their government system entirely. I am confident about this information, however, we lost contact with our operative two weeks ago. At this time, he is presumed dead. I have no way of knowing if our spy was discovered. I also don't know if any information about what has happened in the last two weeks is accurate since my intel is now coming from our operative's informant."

Banji jumped to his feet and started to pace. "You can't let this stand, *Khalon*. An entire planet…how much more are we to allow the Tanis scourge to destroy before we bring them to heel?"

"I will forgive your disrespect given the news of Akia," Ghaleb growled as he stood. "Not that I owe you an explanation, *kijani*, but we are seeking solutions and it will take time. We have not only our planet to consider but galactic consequences to sort out as well."

Banji lowered his head as he sat back down. "Forgive my impertinence."

Ghaleb laid a hand on Banji's shoulder. "I understand your frustration. Concentrate on what we can accomplish now and let me and the others work out the path as we move forward. Our first priority is recovering your brother."

"At least tell me that we will help rebuild what the Tanis have destroyed."

"Do you think Megan would let us do anything less?" Ghaleb retook his seat with a chuckle. Banji smiled.

"Ahm," Kavi coughed. "Back to the mission at hand. My informant located Akia and as of last night he was still alive. We were hoping to figure out a way to extract him without a full blown battle, but those kind of dealings take time. Time is something we no longer have."

"What has changed?" Banji sat forward in his seat, concentrating on the information Kavi was relaying.

"It seems that Daemon, the man controlling Ludus Prime for the Tanis, has concluded that Akia is too much of a liability. The informant says that Daemon plans to get one more big score out of Akia with a last fight."

"I thought he was undefeated?" Ghaleb's brow furrowed.

"If this was a normal fight we would still try to extract him quietly," Kavi said as he placed another crystal tablet on Ghaleb's desk. "It has gone out that there will be a special fight event with a onetime double payout. The catch is Akia's opponent won't be announced until after all of the bets are placed. Most would consider betting on Akia as the victor would be the safe bet, considering his track record." Kavi activated the tablet and a holoimage sprang to life.

"What in the five hells is that?" Banji exclaimed.

"That is a Driak Death Worm," Kavi explained. "They are found only on a large asteroid that was once part of a planet that was destroyed. They decimated every living creature until they were the only things alive on that chunk of rock."

The creature was a huge gelatinous grey body. The only orifice was a mouth filled with hundreds of rows of razor sharp teeth. It was difficult to tell scale in the image until Kavi switched it from a still to video. In the video the creature was fed a rhino-bear, which was easily four times the size of a typical Vukasin warrior.

Its rows of teeth sawed back and forth in its mouth, picking up momentum before it attempted to attack its prey. The rhino-bear fought valiantly to survive, ripping at the worm's flesh. Each time it ripped flesh away, the wound on the Death Worm would close up, healing almost instantly. The creature seemed to ignore the damage its prey was inflicting upon it. The worm arched up before striking the rhino-bear like a snake. The screams of the doomed animal made Banji and Ghaleb wince as it was slowly shredded on its way down the creature's gullet.

Kavi paused the video. "As you can see the thing is almost impossible to kill. In fact, its healing abilities are so advanced that if you bisected the creature you would end up battling two creatures. It is that adaptation that has allowed them to survive when all they have as a food source is each other. Cannibalizing each other doesn't normally kill a Driak Death Worm and only when one creature completely devours another are a new generation of creatures born."

"By the moons are you telling me that the Tanis brought a creature that could possibly destroy an entire planet for a gladiator fight?"

Kavi nodded.

Ghaleb wiped a hand across his face. "How much time do we have?"

"The fight is scheduled for a week from now."

"Any ideas on how we take care of this? Obviously that creature cannot be allowed to run loose."

Kavi leaned back in his chair and steepled his fingers with a sinister smile. "I always have ideas, *Khalon*."

CHAPTER TEN

Akia was dragged from his sleep by the sound of booted feet outside the cell door. He quietly woke Zamira and placed her behind him. A feral growl escaped as the pair listened to the crystal lock being disengaged and the creak of the hinges as the cell door opened.

Akia's first instinct was to charge at the intruders entering his territory; but he fought the urge because he didn't want to leave his mate unprotected. Instead he crouched into a fighting stance, his body shifting until he had teeth and claws at his disposal.

Daemon's soldiers hesitated at the cell door. They had watched the gladiator battles. They knew Akia in his phased form was lethal. After the carnage the beast inflicted they were doubly hesitant to enter his territory.

Akia raised his snout into the air. A deep rumble echoed through Akia's chest and his lip raised in a snarl. Daemon was here. His eyes quickly quartered the enemies before him. In the very back of the group, Akia spotted the man he had vowed to kill.

Daemon scowled at his minions' fear. He raised a boot and shoved the man in front of him sending a domino effect to the front of the line.

"Get on with it!" Daemon barked at his soldiers. "I want the woman."

With those words Akia's roar shook the cell. The sound held almost as much power to influence as Zamira's song did. The soldiers instinctively backed away from the threat. Even Zamira had to fight her natural fight or flight response and she knew that Akia would never hurt her. She couldn't imagine what the soldiers felt knowing he would brutally kill them without a second thought.

"Use the darts!" Daemon's roared order snapped the soldiers out of their fright. They quickly formed a kneeling line with their pulse shields. A second group of soldiers lined up behind the first. Akia remembered what the darts had done to him before. He knew it was likely that they would incapacitate or kill him quickly.

Zamira cried out as Akia exploded into action. He hit the line of pulse shields with the force of a rhino-bear, sending several of the men flying. Once behind the broken line he began a warrior's dance of death. His feet moved quickly while his hands and claws slashed at any opponent near him. Despite his size and the darkness of his actions, Akia's movements were like beautiful poetry, while the Tanis soldiers looked like clumsy idiots. It was no wonder that none could defeat him in a fair battle.

Then the first of the blow darts hit Akia's thigh and he stumbled. The poisons of Ludus Prime were fast acting. Three more darts hit his chest in rapid succession. Akia's movements became slow and uncoordinated but he fought on.

Zamira watched in horror as soldiers were finally able to skirt around Akia to head straight for her. She ran and dodged, but the sparse cell offered nothing in the way of cover. She used the blood-soaked floor to slide between two soldiers but her momentum sent her careening straight into the hands of a third soldier.

He roughly grabbed her arms and hauled her over his shoulder. Her cry of pain had the sluggish Akia turning towards her. He fought the effects of the poison to push his way towards her as the man holding her walked to the door and Daemon.

Zamira reached for Akia from the shoulder of her captor. He could almost touch her fingers when he felt the sting of another dart in his neck. He slowly collapsed to the ground. As Akia's vision faded, the last thing his eyes saw was Zamira screaming and struggling to get to him. It was a futile effort. The Tanis soldier holding her was much stronger and larger than her delicate frame. Akia's final thought before the darkness took his consciousness was, 'Please let her stay safe.'

Zamira watched as Akia quit moving. For a brief moment she was frozen with the fear that he was dead.

"Get him secured before he wakes up." Daemon shoved through the injured soldiers shuffling out of the cell. He eyed Zamira and scowled. "Make sure to double check that the woman hasn't pilfered any of the shackle keys."

Daemon crossed the distance to grabbed Zamira's chin in a bruising grip. "You are going to sing a song of my choosing tonight or lover boy over there dies." He shoved her away from him and shrugged. "I don't particularly care which you choose. I can think of a thousand ways I would enjoy killing that Tiaret scum."

The evil glint in Daemon's eyes told Zamira he was telling the truth. If she didn't sing what he wanted tonight, then Akia would be tortured and killed. She slumped against the shoulder of the man who held her, her head hanging in supposed defeat. She would sing what he told her to sing, for Akia's sake, but that didn't mean she had to put any power behind it.

Daemon chuckled and ordered half his men to move out and the other half to deal with Akia and the mess left behind in their cell.

Tears of regret swam in Zamira's eyes as she stole a final glance of the prone body of the man who had captured her heart. She never even told him how much he meant to her.

*****

Akia woke to a pounding head. He tried to lift his hand to his temple only for it to come up short. He sighed and rolled over onto his back. He was chained to the floor once again. He really wished that they would quit using those twice damned darts. His head felt like one of Megan's ghost-lions was trying to claw its way out of his skull; his body alternated between burning up and shivering until all of the poison finally worked its way out of his system.

If there was an upside it was the fact that it had taken two more darts to knock him out this time. Akia chuckled to himself. If he ever got out of here he was going to be a walking science experiment of strange immunities.

He bolted upright, sending his world into a tail spin. Daemon took Zamira away. His mind must be really foggy because it took a minute or two for Akia to realize that she wasn't in the cell with him. He laid back willing his stomach to settle and the world to stop spinning.

Akia hated this powerless feeling that being a slave had given him. It seemed that no matter how strong and vigilant he was Daemon always had the upper hand. He was beginning to despair of ever being free again. Some days he questioned whether he should just let his next opponent finish him off; but it wasn't just about him anymore. He had to find some way to break free of this cycle of slavery because if he didn't Zamira would be stuck here with him too and that wasn't a future he was willing to accept.

Akia closed his eyes. He could hear the chaos of the casino above. Did any of the patrons spare a thought for those of them caged below? A soft sound flitted above the din of the partying people.

He smiled. Zamira's voice was something he would recognize anywhere, no matter how crowded. The pressure he felt around his heart lifted. He knew she was still alive because if she had died he would have felt the loss in his soul; it was nice to have this confirmation to go along with his faith.

He didn't recognize the song she was singing; it was in Vukasin rather than her native tongue. Her voice also sounded off. It was still impressively beautiful, but it hadn't silenced the masses like other times he heard her sing. The mesmerizing quality it held was missing. Instead of being something magical, her song this night was simply an act by a talented singer.

Akia didn't have the chance to ponder what her song meant for long. The sound of booted feet thumped closer to his cell door. Akia rolled over and crouched. While the chains that shackled his wrists didn't allow for much movement, he refused to meet an enemy while on his back.

"I see you are finally awake," Daemon said, as he pushed through the cell door. A simpering servant trailed behind him with a chair. The servant placed the chair on the floor and Daemon sat, dismissing the man with a wave of his hand.

Akia said nothing. He tracked Daemon's movements with the unblinking stare of a predator. The intensity of that look discomforted Daemon for a moment. He cleared his throat and averted his eyes, his fingers pinching and disposing of a nonexistent piece of lint on his expensively tailored trousers.

"I thought I would do you the courtesy of informing you that you needn't worry about the pretty little song bird after you are gone." Daemon raised his head and looked Akia in the eyes, a lascivious grin on his face. "I plan on taking very good care of her."

Akia lunged for Daemon, the chains jerking him back. His face contorted and his legs shifted.

"I will kill you," Akia snapped with a guttural growl.

Daemon laughed. He had his servant place his chair just outside of the reach of the chains. He was confident that gave him the control here.

"After tomorrow night you won't have a say either way." He tapped his chin thoughtfully, "I know. I'll bring your little woman so she can watch your death before I have my way with her. I've been far too lenient and look where that has gotten me." Daemon sighed dramatically. He leaned forward with an evil grin. "And the best part is, if you don't walk willingly to your doom, I will kill your woman and I will make sure she suffers a long time before being granted the peace of death."

Daemon's smiled slipped as Akia strained against his chains. The color leeched from his face with the first popping sound. The chains were fastened to a metal plate on the floor by a half dozen bolts. One went flying as the stone floor cracked around it. The crack widened to include two more bolts.

Daemon scrambled from his chair and pounded on the door of the cell calling for the guard to open it. He scurried out of the cell and slammed the door shut just as Akia pulled the final bolt free with a roar. Daemon leaned against it thankful that he escaped in time. It just confirmed his decision to take the future loss of bets and do away with the troublesome Tiaret.

Akia hit the door with enough force to knock Daemon down to his knees. There was a noticeable dent in the thick metallic door. Daemon yelled at the stunned guard to get men down there to reinforce the door so the slave didn't escape.

If he had his way, he would just gas Akia's entire cell until it killed the bastard. But the announcement for the fight had gone out weeks ago and the bets were already rolling in. Daemon had one last round of bets to get out of the Vukasin Beast; he wanted to milk as many credits from it as he could. Daemon stood to make a fortune, not only from those betting on the Vukasin Beast as the victor but from his own personal bet placed on the "mystery" opponent.

CHAPTER ELEVEN

Daemon paced the room he had created as his office. Luxurious rugs, fine fabrics, and expensive furniture filled the space. It was a room fit for a king. He pulled the rare Ludus liquor from the discreet bar he kept next to his desk.

Getting rid of the Tiaret was an easy decision, but what to do with the priestess was more complicated. He could easily intimidate her physically and her voice brought in almost as many credits as the Tiaret did. But the glimpse of power he saw the night she stopped Akia's rampage frightened him in a way the beast did not.

With a single sound she had frozen not only Daemon but an entire arena of people. She had the power to stop an entire army if she chose to use it. Daemon shivered. He had never believed in magic before coming to this backwater planet; but he couldn't deny the priestess's power. It made him wonder what the other priestesses were capable of.

Part of him wished he had been able to harness that power for himself. If he had he could have challenged even Bel himself for control of the entire Tanis empire. But he was intelligent enough to know that ship had sailed. She had bonded with the Tiaret beast, making both of them even more dangerous than they were before.

A knock sounded on his office door.

"Enter."

"My lord, you wanted a report of tonight's numbers."

Daemon tipped another drink of the strong alcoholic beverage to his lips while gesturing for his underling to continue.

The timid man shuffled through a few screens on

his crystal tablet before settling on the information he wanted. "Revenue was good, but there wasn't a noticeable increase in gambling even with the priestess singing. However, there wasn't a break in gambling which usually happens during her performance. The set did receive good reviews from patrons but not the visceral emotional reactions as was the case in the past."

Daemon finished his drink and placed the glass on the corner of his desk. "That will be all."

The underling bowed and exited the office.

"Damn the five hells," Daemon said to himself. He would have to get rid of the woman. If forcing her to sing the songs of his choice doesn't have the same mesmerizing effect, then she was just a liability. After the death of the Tiaret beast he would have no leverage to control her. He had no doubt that she would use the paralyzing aspect of her voice to destroy him. It would be in his best interest to get rid of her quickly.

He knew that the natives would revolt if he outright killed their priestess. He didn't worry about them overpowering his men. The Tanis were superior in both physical prowess and technology. They could easily wipe out the local population. No, Daemon worried about the loss of revenue from the slave sales. There were numerous species that craved the delicate femininity that permeated the citizens of Ludus Prime. There was even a market for the delicate males of this planet.

Daemon would be losing two of his biggest credit makers with the death of the woman and her beast; he refused to take another blow to his personal fortunes. The priestess's death had to look like an accident to prevent a revolt.

Decision made, Daemon returned to planning his next moves. The next few days would be critical.

CHAPTER TWELVE

Tonight was the night. Not being able to sleep next to Zamira, now that he had had a taste of her soft warmth, was a worse torture than anything else he had suffered at Daemon's hands. Akia added that sin to the long lists of reasons why Daemon needed to die.

He heard booted feet nearing his door. The number seemed quite small for what was usually sent to escort him to the arena. Of course Daemon knew that with the threats to Zamira's safety should he not show at the fight guaranteed his cooperation.

The guards came to retrieve Akia. He did not fight or try to intimidate them despite the stench of their obvious fear. There were three of them. Akia hated how sure of himself and this night Daemon was; but he couldn't do anything about it now. The outcome of this bout was too important to waste energy on Daemon's underlings.

Akia blocked out everything but the instinct to survive. He still didn't know who or what he was fighting; but he knew that Daemon was certain he wouldn't survive the battle.

Defeat wasn't an option. He would kill anything placed in front of him if it meant surviving. He wouldn't leave Zamira in the hands of someone like Daemon. He pushed all thoughts from his mind. He became like stone, unfeeling and immovable. Only time could defeat him and Daemon didn't have enough time. Akia's breathing slowed as he fell deeper into the warrior's meditation. He was centered and ready.

His beast pushed closer to the surface. Akia allowed his senses take on the strength of the beast but he kept iron control. Whatever enemy Daemon had found for him, he knew that mindless savagery would not win the day.

His guards stopped him at the arena doors. Two

of the three guards left, shutting the gate behind them. The last one was just a young whelp barely out of his warrior's den. He didn't leave but shifted nervously next to Akia. Akia could have easily killed the kid, but it wouldn't matter. He wouldn't get past the arena gates. Even if he managed to break down the reinforced doors, there was a platoon of guards stationed outside with orders to kill anything that came through those gates. He had discovered that during previous battles. Only his status as a credit maker had saved him in the past, it wouldn't now. So he ignored the young man and waited for the doors to the arena to open to his fate.

"Um…"

Akia gave the youngster a side-eyed glance but said nothing.

"I saw what they are sending you up against." The kid pulled an energy blade that he had stashed inside of his boot and held it out to Akia. "What they are doing isn't right. I can't stop the fight, but I can at least try to help, though it probably won't do much." That last part the soldier said in defeat under his breath.

"Thanks." Akia reached for the energy blade but dropped it as he hit his knees clutching his head.

Akia! Damn you to the five hells, answer me!

Turn down the frexing volume, Banji.

It had been over a year since Akia and Banji were able to communicate telepathically and it was putting a strain on Akia.

Finally. We have been trying to reach you since we hit planet side three nights ago. Where are you?

I'm about to enter the arena for a fight Daemon is confident will kill me.

Damn. He's right. They got this thing called a Driak Death Worm. Frexing thing is practically immortal, you can't kill it. But we have a plan, just keep away from it until we get there. Akia could hear his brother sigh in his mind. *I'm not going to lie, it will take some time for us to get to you. We still have to find a way to get to the arena without raising the alarm.*

Hold on for a minute, Akia replied.

Akia looked at the kid who was trying to help him get to his feet.

"What clan are you, boy?" Akia scooped up the blade and stood back up.

"Tanis. Th…the elites came to our village and forced every able bodied male into the military whether they wanted to join or not. My uncle was killed when he resisted. I haven't seen any one else from the village since our training was completed."

"If you could get away from the Tanis would you go?"

"Go where? None of the other clans would take a Tanis male."

"Just answer the question."

"Yes. I want no part in whatever new hell the elites are creating. I just want to go back to being a simple farmer, like my family always has been."

Banji, I've got you an inside man. We would have to take him with us after this. Where can you meet him? He might be helpful.

South gate of the arena. We have already made it into the city. We are hoping to blend in with the other spectators, but some of us need to smuggle in our little surprise. If your man could get us through without raising the alarm it would help immensely.

"What's your name, boy?"

"Jax."

"Well, Jax, if you want out from under the Tanis thumb I may be able to help, but you will have to help me first."

Jax looked dubious. "What would you need me to do?"

"Go to the south gate. There are some people

there who might be able to use your help. You help them and they will take you off this rock and you can just be a farmer again."

"How do you know this?"

"It doesn't really matter how, I just do. Time is running short so I need to know whether or not you will help me. Choose your side wisely, Jax. What you choose to do in this moment will define your future."

Jax thought about what Akia said and nodded. "Anything has to be better that not having a choice. I'll accept your offer."

"Good, you have my gratitude."

"Don't thank me yet, I don't know if anything I can do will make a difference."

Akia tested the balance of the energy blade and shrugged. "We can only do what we can do, Jax. You never know when a small action will change the course of history."

Banji, he's on his way. Be prepared for him and an additional passenger for extraction.

I think we can handle that, Akia.

Jax nodded, Akia almost missed the gesture. He had to get used to splitting his attention again.

The young man started to walk away but turned before he reached the gate. "This is fight night. There are thousands of people coming in and out of all the gates. How do I know which people to talk to?"

Akia laughed, hope building up in his chest that he might be able to get Zamira safely away from here. "Just look for the guy who looks like me, only prettier."

CHAPTER THIRTEEN

Zamira ignored the women as they fussed around her. She was used to having someone dress her from her time in the temple. But she found that since her enslavement she preferred to dress herself since the only time someone dressed her was when she had to play the part of a pretty decoration on Daemon's arm.

Tonight Daemon had been almost gleeful when he led the other women into her cell with his selection of clothes for the evening. Three women trailed after him. One was carrying a scrap of material the same color as her amethyst eyes that she assumed was her dress. Another carried a basket filled with hair dressing items and the gold and purple Ayayi orchids found only near her temple home. The final woman carried a case filled with make-up supplies. Daemon was almost nice with the women, smiling at them as he directed them in how he wanted Zamira to look.

Daemon was acting out of character. Zamira's intuition screamed that he seemed way too happy about something and her thoughts immediately went to Akia. She knew Akia had a gladiatorial battle; it was why she was being dressed like a doll after all. Daemon didn't dare leave her behind after the carnage Akia wrought during her last absence. The only things that made Daemon smile were amassing credits and hurting people. Zamira had a feeling that tonight probably entailed both.

Zamira gasped as one of the attendants tightened the lacing of her dress's bodice. She shoved the woman away.

"I doubt Daemon would be happy if I end up passing out from a lack of oxygen."

The poor woman paled, making Zamira almost feel bad for scaring her. Zamira turned her back to the fussing women. Thankfully someone loosened the ties so she could breathe again.

There wasn't a mirror in Zamira's cell but judging by what she could see looking down Daemon had chosen yet another tacky and revealing dress to parade her around in. Her breasts were thrust high thanks to the tight lacing. Her skirt, if one could call it that, was composed of several ruffled strips that bared her legs when she walked. The sleeves were made from sheer material that attached at the wrist but slide off her shoulder. It was an outfit that Zamira felt would have been right at home in a brothel. Honestly, the man seemed to think that attractive only meant practically naked.

"Ow!" Zamira glared at another woman who had been applying make-up. The idiot had poked her eye while applying some garish color on her face. Zamira closed her eyes and took a deep breath. Violence would solve nothing, but she didn't have to put up with the abuse. Zamira snatched the compact from the woman's hand. "That is enough. Thank you." The woman started to protest but the priestess had perfected her icy glare years ago. Eventually the woman just curtsied and moved to wait by the cell door.

As the other two women finished dressing her hair, Zamira sighed. These women were as much prisoners as she was. It wasn't fair to take her ill temper out on them. But Zamira was finding it difficult to act the part of magnanimous religious leader when all she cared about was figuring out what Daemon had planned.

Her instincts were telling her that whatever had put Daemon in such a good mood was bad news for Akia and herself.

"Do any of you know who the Vukasin Beast is battling tonight?"

One woman made the final adjustments to her hair, placing the last of the Ayayi orchids so that the flowers seemed to tumble around her neck and down her shoulders following the cascade of her midnight hair, that had been plaited into several intricate braids and artfully arranged.

When she stepped back to survey her work she said, "The challenger is being kept secret. They are even forcing the gamblers to bet blind, mistress." She patted Zamira's arm like a mother might to a child. "Do not worry. According to the odds being given, most people still expect your beast to win."

Zamira started to say something when she heard the sound of the crystal lock disengaging. Daemon opened her cell door and ushered the other women out to a group of waiting guards.

"Come, my little song bird." Daemon held out his hand to Zamira. She knew better than to defy him even though the touch of his hand made her skin crawl. *This is for Akia's sake, not my own*, she repeated over and over in her mind. He placed her hand in the crook of his arm. The casual observer would think that she accompanied him by choice.

Daemon walked down the corridor with Zamira. Instead of taking their usual route to the arena, he ushered her to a lift. Zamira could feel his eyes on her after the lift took off. The highly polished metallic walls allowed her to see him without turning to face him. His face held a malevolent grin and lust was evident in his eyes. She had seen him look at some of the other women that way and it never ended well for the woman.

She had thought that between her voice and Akia that she was safe from that kind of speculation. If Daemon was looking at her as his next personal entertainment, then Zamira knew that he didn't expect Akia to be around much longer. She had to keep her eyes and ears open, as one never knew when a piece of information would become valuable.

The doors of the lift opened onto the casino floor. Even though Zamira had often sung in the lounge on this level she had never actually been allowed access to the casino. The lights and sounds were dizzying. Everywhere you turned people were drowning in excess.

To the untrained eye it was hedonism and pleasure at its finest. But Zamira was a priestess of Ti'lak. Beneath the surface she saw the loneliness and desperation of those that laughed the hardest. She watched as beautiful woman after beautiful woman plodded after their boisterous targets with hopeless eyes. She saw individual after individual try to fill a hole in their soul with credits and alcohol that would never be filled. She couldn't suppress a shiver from all of the negative emotions flowing around her.

"Are you cold, little song bird?"

Zamira shook her head and Daemon returned his attention to the casino floor.

The song swelling in her heart begged for her to reveal to the masses that they were chasing shallow things that will never make them happy. But she kept silent for now. Daemon would surely kill her if she cleared his casino. She waited and listened.

Daemon led her to a raised platform in the center of the casino floor.

"How are the numbers?" Daemon asked one of his minions in front of a holo-display.

"It is the largest take yet, Lord Daemon."

"Excellent. Make the announcement that betting closes in ten minutes and the opponent will be revealed in the arena."

"Yes, my lord."

"Put another two million of my personal credits down on the opponent as the winner."

"Do you want that in addition to the eight million in casino funds you have already placed?"

"Yes."

Daemon's minion punched in the numbers onto his crystal tablet. "Are you sure you want to tie up that much of the casino's funds, sir? If the Vukasin Beast wins it will almost bankrupt operations."

Daemon grabbed the man's tablet, crushing the poor idiot's fingers in the process. "I don't pay you to question me." He tossed the tablet back onto the table. "Just make sure that the winnings from both bets are deposited into my personal account at the end of the night."

Zamira's face paled at Daemon's confidence. She knew that this was a death match. Every battle Daemon had forced Akia into since his rampage had been a fight to the death. If anyone knew just how hard it was to kill Akia, it was Daemon. For him to be so certain of this match's outcome that he would bet not only his own fortune but risk the wrath of Bel by betting the casino's credits made Zamira nervous. Just who or what was Akia up against?

Daemon turned to a man at a separate display. "What do production numbers look like?"

"We are on schedule for the delivery to Bel. The Kassis order is behind schedule, something about genetic anomalies tainting the first batch."

"Make sure they know that if they can't deliver on schedule they will end up in the area as fodder for the fighters."

"Yes, my lord."

Zamira   frowned.   Delivery…genetics?
Everywhere she turned there seemed to be more
questions than answers. What the hell was happening
on her own planet?

CHAPTER FOURTEEN

"You must be Jax."

Banji leaned casually against the wall near the entrance to the arena.

"He wasn't kidding when he said you looked like him." Jax looked Banji up and down. He was obviously related to the Vukasin Beast. Both of their faces carried the dark hair characteristic of almost all Vukasin people. However, both men's eyes were a strange shade of dark blue. Blue eyes were extremely rare on Vukas. Even if their eyes had been different colors, the shape of their faces could have been mirror images. Though the man standing before him wasn't as muscular as the gladiator he had just left. Jax knew that had more to do with the drugs the elites pumped into their fighters than anything else. "Can you really get me away from the Tanis?"

"When we leave this rock, we will take you with us. That was the agreement for your help and we Tiarets always keep our word."

Jax considered what the man in front of him said; at this point he had nothing to lose. His soul was dying a little at a time the longer he stayed here. If he died trying to escape so be it.

"I need to know what all you need; but we need to hurry. The fight starts in just a few minutes and I am not sure how long The Beast can last."

"Akia…his name is Akia of the clan Tiaret."

"Oh," Jax ran a hand through his hair and looked down sheepishly. "He never gave me his name."

"Did you ask for it?"

Jax blushed and Banji realized how young the boy was. "No, I suppose I didn't."

"He's my brother. I'm Banji by the way." Banji pulled Jax into the shadows as a group of spectators walked by. "I need to get to the arena floor. Those two," he waved at a couple of military men behind him, "need to be up somewhere high with a good view of the arena floor."

"I can take you down through the holding cells. They open up right onto the arena." Jax stopped to think about where to put the men who needed to be up high. "There is a service walkway across the roof of the arena building. The middle would have a clear view of the arena below but I don't know if we can use it."

"Why not? It sounds perfect."

"There are always men stationed up there for troubleshooting lights and sound. There are also a few soldiers that patrol that area for crowd control."

"Get my men to the walkway's access and we will take care of the rest."

Banji gave Jax a feral grin. For the first time the man in front of him truly looked like the Vukasin Beast to Jax. The men loyal to the royal house of Ivalio may be more fair in their dealings with others but only a fool would forget that they are fierce and skilled warriors.

"Can you cover your face somehow?" Jax asked Banji. "Your brother is somewhat of a celebrity around here even if he is a slave. The last thing we need is someone to mistake you for him."

Banji drew his hood over his head and raised a scarf to cover the bottom half of his face. He couldn't do anything about his unusual blue eyes. Thankfully in the shadows they were so dark that they almost appeared to be black.

When Jax was satisfied that Banji had concealed his looks well enough he began to lead the contingent of men through the back hallways of the arena complex. As they moved deeper into the bowels of the building Jax stopped at a small unmarked door. He opened it to reveal a maintenance closet. Jax pulled various mops and brooms and handed them out to the group of men behind him.

Banji looked at the mop in his hand and raised a questioning eyebrow when Jax also handed him a bucket.

"This place isn't high-tech enough for automated cleaning. I think Daemon likes people to do the manual labor because it gives him a sense of power. They are always adding new people to the cleaning crews so no one will question it if they don't recognize you. Plus, they would fully expect to see a lowly soldier such as myself leading you around to teach you what your duties are. Just keep your head down and look dejected."

"You are a smart man, Jax." Banji clapped him on the back. "Are you sure you just want to be a farmer when we get back?"

"How did you know…? Never mind. We need to get moving if you are going to be in place before the fight starts."

CHAPTER FIFTEEN

Daemon walked into his VIP area. It was a platform raised above the masses. There were several such platforms for the wealthiest gamblers of the casino. Not only were the seats much more luxurious, every vice imaginable was available to the patrons.

Zamira could see the women of her planet dressed in barely there dresses. Granted the material was of the highest quality. It was so fine that you could see through it, which was probably the point. The women kept the patrons supplied with whatever their credits could pay for. Unfortunately, for the women serving the VIP platforms that included themselves.

Zamira bit her lip to keep from crying out as she watched a young woman pulled into the lap of a lecherous old man. She had to avert her eyes when the woman's protests were met with violence. She could hear the other males on the platform laughing at the woman's distress. *How could people do such horrible things to other people?* She would never understand it.

"Patrons of Paradise Casinos!" a loud voice echoed across the arena.

 The lights in the stands lowered while the arena floor lit up with strobing lights in a multitude of colors. Daemon designed the spectacle to make the paying guests forget that the people and creatures in the arena weren't there by choice. The theatrics made it feel like this was simply a performance with superstars and up and comers rather than slaves and prisoners.

Three different fights were scheduled for that night. Akia's would be the last battle fought.

Zamira glanced sideways at Daemon. The man was practically bouncing in his seat. She wished she could get one of the workers alone to see if they had any idea who Akia's opponent would be.

She moved over to the bar area at the back of Daemon's platform. He didn't have servers coming and going, instead everything he could want was already at his fingertips. Zamira knew that is was Daemon's subtle way of informing the patrons that he was above them. Of course Daemon didn't understand that his wealthy patrons didn't care about his displays of power as long as he continued to serve them their distractions like the servant they viewed him as.

"Bring me a glass of the Hyanth Liquor," Daemon snapped at Zamira. He wasn't as oblivious to her as he seemed to be.

Zamira poured his drink. A part of her wished she could poison the damn thing but that wasn't an option at the moment. Maybe she could get him pass out drunk so she could make her escape. She brought the drink to the rim of the glass. She opted for water for herself. Zamira wanted to make sure that her senses remained sharp. Her instincts were screaming at her that quick action might be the only thing between her and disaster.

Walking carefully so as not to spill the expensive alcohol, Zamira made her way back to the seats at the front of the platform. She handed Daemon his drink as the announcer called out the first fight. This was a new pair of slaves. If they gave a good show, they may both survive another day since the audience got to vote on what happened to the defeated fighter. Daemon had found that killing one of his fighters during every round was costly since he would have to be replaced. It was a fairly shrewd move to give the audience a vote since it made them feel a part of the show. Plus Daemon could always rig the vote counts for whatever outcome he wanted whenever he felt like it.

Unfortunately for the young fighter who fell, tonight both Daemon and the crowd were rather bloodthirsty. His death was voted in with a roaring cheer from the crowd. Zamira turned away as the other fighter gave the death blow.

The second battle was a group of the deformed phased. These were once Vukasin men who had been experimented on. They were injected with many of the same drugs that they pumped into Akia. Unlike Akia who had managed to keep control, those men had changed into their beasts and were unable to change back. The muscle and strength enhancing formulas distorted their bodies as the scientists continued to try new combinations. They were now wild, rabid animals led by the instinct to survive and kill.

Their pack mentality made them perfect for pitting against other apex predators. Tonight five of the deformed phased were facing five different deadly creatures from their home planet...a pair of shesha serpents with their deadly venom that were large enough that they could devour a man, two rhino-bears with their plate-like armor and horns, and lastly the majestic ghost-lion -a cunning hunter

107

known throughout numerous planets.

Zamira watched in fascinated horror as the pack of the deformed phased culled one of the rhino-bears from the other animals. They used their claws to cut the tendons on the animal's rear legs. The huge creature fell to the ground with a crash that seemed to shake the floor. Even in their rabid state the deformed phased showed their instinctual hunting strategies. They quickly dispatched the fallen rhino-bear and used the enormous body to shield themselves from the other creatures.

One of the deformed phase that ripped out the throat of the rhino-bear seemed to fall into an eating frenzy. The alpha of the pack snarled and pushed him away from the carcass, staking his claim. The other pack member growled and bared his fangs as if in challenge but eventually exposed his throat in a sign of submission. However, treachery can occur even within a pack. As the alpha turned to face the attack of the other rhino-bear, he was jumped from behind by the pack member he had just reprimanded. Caught between two opponents, the alpha quickly fell.

The gloating traitor howled his victory only to have it cut off by the strike of the shesha. The serpent dragged its prize off to a corner to devour him. A strangled cry was heard from the smallest pack member as the other shesha wrapped him in coils and squeezed the life out of him. Zamira knew from watching previous bouts with the shesha that the creatures will eat the opponent and then fall into almost a stupor as they digest them. They can move if threatened, but they will no longer seek out prey.

As the serpents ate their comrades the two remaining pack members were able to take down the final rhino-bear, but the battle had cost them. They were bleeding from several gashes and one of them had an arm flopping useless at his side. The poor deformed phased still had to contend with the ghost-lion who had prowled the perimeter of the arena. Zamira could swear that the great cat had purposely kept out of the fray to wear down its prey. Those cunning eyes now tracked the two remaining pack members. It seemed to be calculating the odds, as it stalked them. Its gaze reminded her a bit of Akia. They were both apex predators. A few steps and then it would freeze, the tips of its double tail the only thing that moved. Then it would take a few more steps.

The suspense caused the crowd to hush as they watched and waited. Suddenly the cat burst into motion, launching itself over the body of the rhino-bear. Midflight its giant claws swiped across the throat of the deformed with the useless arm. The crowd bust into roaring cheers as the poor creature gurgled with wide eyes, drowning in his own blood. The ghost-lion ignored the dying opponent and turned to face his final prey.

Even from a distance, Zamira could see the resignation in the deformed phase's eyes. With a defiant war cry he launched himself at the ghost-lion. His jaw locked onto the ghost-lion's neck, though the cat's armor plating prevented a killing blow. He held on for dear life and raked his claws along the ghost-lion's side trying to get to his soft underbelly. Even with the strength enhancing drugs the wounded phased was no match for the sheer bulk of the ghost-lion, who rolled and crushed the man beneath him. In a matter of moments, the giant cat dispatched the final dazed deformed phased.

Since neither the ghost-lion or the sheshas seemed the least bit interested in each other, the battle was declared over and intermission was called. The next battle would be Akia's.

CHAPTER SIXTEEN

Be careful, brother. Five minutes can be a lifetime in battle.

The corner of Akia's mouth lifted. It wasn't that long ago that he was the one worrying about Banji. It seems that time had reversed their roles somewhat.

By the moons you sure have become a worrywart. I told you I would hold out until you came to the rescue.

Intermission was over and Akia could hear the muffled voice of the announcer. He also heard the audience start roaring defiantly when they heard that he would be battling the practically immortal Driak Death Worm. There was a real possibility that Daemon could have a riot on his hands.

That is my cue. Just hurry up and play the hero.

The doors of his holding cell opened onto the arena. Akia didn't bother to hide the energy blade that Jax had given him. Besides he didn't want to waste precious seconds trying to fish it out of a hiding spot.

Akia walked out onto the arena floor. Directly across from him he saw a huge set of doors.

"Well that's new," he mumbled to himself.

He raised his nose to the air and scented. It was faint, but underneath the odor of the masses, the faint floral scent he recognized as Zamira was there. His eyes shifted to Daemon's platform. She was there, watching white knuckled at the railing. Even when Daemon tried to pull her away, she shrugged him off. There was no way Akia was going to allow himself to die in front of his mate. He had to survive so he could keep his promise to get them both away from here. His brother was here to help; it would be his only opportunity with a real chance of success; but only if he could survive the next few minutes.

The ponderous metallic doors' locking mechanism shifted and hissed until popping free. Slowly they creaked open as the spectators held their breath. As the doors spread open an energy shield raised between the arena floor and the audience.

"That can't be good."

For a moment nothing happened. Then a screeching roar followed by the interrupted yell of a man echoed through the space. In the shadows of the doors something moved. Light glinted off a grey gelatinous body that filled the entire opening. By the gods, that things almost filled the arena.

Akia's eyes traveled up the creature's body. There didn't seem to be any appendages or even eyes. The only thing that denoted head from tail was the circular mouth with row upon row of teeth. Teeth which were at that moment blood stained and had a pair of mangled legs hanging from them. That was probably the scream they heard earlier.

Akia called upon his beast and phased. He would need the quicker reflexes of his animal side since the sheer size of his opponent left little room for maneuvering. Thanks to Banji he knew trying to kill this thing was a waste of time. He just needed to survive long enough for help to get there.

Fight smarter, not harder was what Kavi used to tell them in training. Akia watched the Death Worm as it snapped at the energy field causing the

spectators behind to scream in terror.   While its
forward movement was slow, the speed of its attack
was impressive.

The logical choice would be to get behind the
creature and shadow its movements until the cavalry
came. But, Akia knew that if Daemon suspected that
he knew about the nature of this creature he would
attack using other methods because Daemon had
made it clear that he didn't want Akia to leave the
arena alive. So he had to make the show look good
while avoiding being eaten.

Akia turned the energy blade up. It was a smaller
blade so even at its highest setting he ended up only
with a short sword. The crowd murmured. Weapons
had never been allowed in the gladiator's hands.
Those in the audience who know of his reputation
and that of the Driak Death Worm hoped for the first
time since the opponent announcement that their bets
on the Vukasin Beast as the victor might still bear
fruit. The worm might be nearly immortal, but the
Vukasin Beast was death walking.

A few members of the audience started jumping
up and down. The Death Worm stuck the energy
field near them. The creature seemed to be attracted
to movement. The spectators in that area screamed
and crawled over each other to get away as the worm
repeatedly struck the energy field. May the gods
help them if that thing breaks through.

Akia used his opponent's distraction to move

around the back of the creature. Daemon saw Akia skirting around and scowled when his eyes met Akia's glare. Daemon grabbed Zamira and yanked her close. Akia could hear her cry of surprise and pain. Daemon mimed cutting a throat and looked pointedly at Zamira before returning his gaze to Akia and pointing at the worm. Akia got the message loud and clear: engage in battle or Zamira suffers.

Hey little brother, I need you to hurry up on the rescue operation.

Akia could feel Banji's chuckle in his mind. *You are going to constantly bring up the fact that you were born a few minutes ahead of me aren't you?*

Focus please.

Our men are moving onto the walk way above as we speak. I'm in the holding cell area. Jax has left to open the door so I can meet you on the arena floor. We need to rendezvous with the extraction team in half an hour.

Got it.

"Time to put on a show." Akia raised his energy blade and gave a loud war cry as he ran up the back of the gigantic Death Worm. At the top of the head he plunged the blade into the area that logic says would house the creature's brain.

The crowd went wild when the worm let out a

grating shriek of pain. In any other creature that move would have been a death blow but to the Driak Death Worm it just seemed to piss it off. The creature thrashed and screamed, trying to dislodge Akia from the back of its head. Akia pulled the blade to plunge it once more into the creature's head and watched in fascinated horror as the wound he just inflicted disappeared before his eyes.

The worm twisted and bucked in the moment of Akia's hesitation. The motion sent him flying across the arena. Akia shook his head as his world tilted on its axis. He flexed his arms and legs and noticed he somehow retained hold of the energy blade. Good there were no broken bones but he was going to need a regen unit for the bruising.

Out of the corner of his eye he saw the death worm turn in his direction. *Frex*, it was zeroing in on his movement. Akia stilled when every survival instinct screamed at him to get as far away as he could. The cunning warrior within fought his animal side for control. The warrior knew that this creature couldn't see him in the same way as other creatures could as it had no eyes. In fact, Akia couldn't see any sensory organs but the Death Worm still reacted to movement, even behind the energy shield. So more likely than not the creature's entire body was a sensory organ of sorts. It probably felt the very subtle kinetic waves that body movement sent through the air. The energy field might distort those waves but it couldn't stop them entirely because the energy field wave was a wave itself; unless it was oscillating at exactly the right frequency to cancel out the movement of the spectators, some residual wave would have to make it through.

Really? Do you have to give yourself a science lecture when faced with almost certain death?

Well, I was getting bored waiting on you to get here and do your frexing job, Banji.

The worm turned back to attack the energy field as the audience cheered and generally caused a ruckus.

I've got to make this look good or Daemon will take me out the old fashioned way. So I would appreciate it if you hurried your ass up.

Well, glad to see somethings never change. You are as bossy as ever. I'll be there in two minutes. When you see me, get away from that thing as fast as you can.

Akia launched himself once more at the back of the worm. This time he used his claws on one hand to dig into the creature's flesh so he could hold on while the other hand plunged the energy blade repeatedly into the creature. He knew this was all for show as the wounds healed almost instantly. Even when his claws were buried into the creature, the area around his fingers healed. He was going to have to rip his hand from beneath the flesh when he made his escape.

The crowd went wild as Akia rode the bucking worm like a cowboy on a bronco from the Earth films his brother used to watch. Akia laughed out loud when the worm tried to dislodge him once again. It had been so long that he had almost forgotten what it was like to have his brother in his life.

"Ride 'em, cowboy!" Akia whooped at the crowd.

CHAPTER SEVENTEEN

Zamira couldn't feel her fingers any longer, but she didn't care. They would have to pry her hands from the railing to get her to leave the arena. Her horror deepened when she realized that despite numerous direct hits by Akia, the Driak Death Worm remained undamaged. No wonder Daemon was particularly cheerful this evening.

She chanced a glance in the casino king's direction. He seemed amused and distracted by the spectacle in the arena. Zamira turned her gaze back to the man who held her heart. He was avoiding the creature's giant maw by staying attached to the back of its head. But the worm's thrashing would eventually dislodge Akia, making him easy prey.

Zamira knew that she could mesmerize the audience but she had never encountered a creature like the Driak Death Worm before. She wasn't even sure the creature's brain was complex enough to recognize her music.

She was so focused on Akia that she almost missed the roar that started building in the crowd.

"Two of them?"

"I knew the Beast's record was too good to be true."

"How many credits did they cheat us out of?"

Then she saw him. On the other side of the arena there was a man who had Akia's face; but he lacked the hardness of Akia's demeanor.

The masses were no longer interested in the fight below, though it was the only thing that mattered to Zamira. She couldn't care less if the crowd attacked Daemon. As far as she was concerned it was the least he deserved. In fact, there was a dark part of her that hoped the crowd ripped him to pieces.

'Where's the calm forgiving priestess now?' her inner voice taunted. She shut it out. If she learned any lesson in this time as a slave, it was that there are some men who are just evil and you have no power to redeem them. Daemon was one such man. More than one world would be better off if he were dead.

Someone in the crowd screamed. Her eyes snapped back to the Death Worm's head just in time to see Akia flying through the air, hitting the wall, and landing with an audible thump on the arena floor. He laid there not moving.

Zamira stood up straight and took a deep breath. She had to try to save Akia and she had only one weapon at her disposal. Zamira opened her mouth to release one pure tone into the entire arena, but before the sound could climb from her diaphragm, rough hands grabbed her from behind and stuffed her mouth with cloth until she nearly choked. Her hands were quickly bound behind her back.

"Did you really think I would let you get away with your little trick again?" Daemon stalked closer to Zamira with an evil smirk on his face. "If I'm lucky both of the Tiaret twins will die in the arena tonight. But it doesn't matter." He grabbed her face and dragged her close. "It's time to use my exit strategy. After tonight someone else can manage this rock."

Zamira tried to free her head from his bruising grip as he licked the side of her face. "It really is too bad you had to fall for the beast. I had such plans for you. I should have sampled you when I had the chance." Daemon chuckled and sighed dramatically.

Zamira knew that Daemon didn't plan on her living through the night. She could see it in his eyes. She pulled at the restraints. It was times like these she wished she had Akia's physical strength.

Daemon suddenly scowled and threw Zamira to the ground and rushed to the railing of the platform.

"What in the five hells?"

Zamira scooted her body across the platform floor until she could look through the railings to the arena below. Akia was up and moving with his twin as beams of fiery light rained down from above.

The beams were directed at the Driak Death Worm. As they passed over its flesh, huge chunks just seemed to vaporize. It was horrifying but Zamira couldn't look away.

Zamira could hear Daemon shouting orders to his soldiers to get whoever was up on the walk way. A bomb exploded on the other side of the arena and Akia's twin was trying to drag his brother towards it.

Zamira knew Akia hesitated because he was looking for her. She tried to cry out to him but the sound was muffled by the cloth in her mouth. She thrashed to get his attention.

Daemon screamed in frustrated rage as the individuals above finally figured out that to defeat the death worm they would have to systematically burn it away from all directions to prevent regeneration.

Akia looked up at the platform and his eyes connected with Zamira's. He had let his beast fully take over as Daemon's soldiers poured into the arena. Akia's strength and agility were a beautiful dance of death as he fought his way to her. She could hear his twin yelling that they had to get out of here now, but Akia was focused only on getting to Zamira.

Daemon grabbed the bindings securing Zamira's arms and lifted her up to dangle above the floor. The pressure on her shoulders as she hung there was excruciating. Daemon smirked as she screamed behind her gag.

"Well it seems you will live a bit longer, little song bird. I have use for you still."

He slung her over his shoulder and calmly walked away from the chaos of the arena. He barked orders at his minions as he passed by. That was how she knew he was taking her away from the slave cells to his personal fortress, where he would lay in wait for Akia.

"You are my insurance policy. Before I leave this gods forsaken rock I will kill your precious beast."

Zamira jumped as he slapped her on her backside. "Don't worry, little priestess. You won't have to live with the guilt of causing his death for very long. That I can promise you."

CHAPTER EIGHTEEN

Akia heard the yells accusing Daemon of cheating from the audience first. After all it was taking everything he had just to stay seated on the bucking Death Worm. He lifted his gaze to see his brother finally entering the arena.

Akia ripped his clawed hand from the healed flesh of the worm and prepared to shimmy down the creature like they had planned. The worm had other ideas though. It reared up higher than any of its previous moves and slug its head to the side with such force that Akia went flying. The wall of the arena stopped his rapid acceleration and he crashed to the floor. His vision tunneled and his arms trembled to the point that they couldn't support his weight.

"That's all right. I'll just lay here for a bit," the befuddled Akia said to himself. The beast within growled as survival instincts as old as time kicked in. He pushed himself off of the floor, nearly gutting Banji as he tried to help him up.

"Come on, old man. The fireworks are about to start and we need to get out of here." Banji pulled at Akia's arm, trying to direct him away from Daemon's platform and Zamira.

Akia ignored the fire of light that rained down on the worm. He ignored the blast that opened a huge hole in the arena wall. His mate was on the platform with Daemon and he would not leave without her.

Daemon shouted orders over the railing as hatred burned in his eyes. Tanis soldiers swarmed the arena floor as the worm evaporated with an ear piercing scream in a cloud of charred flesh. Akia watched as Daemon lifted Zamira high into the air and then slung her over his shoulder.

Akia rushed the platform as Daemon walked away only to be stopped by a squad of soldiers. He let the beast's rage at his mate being taken from him by another male boil to the surface. Teeth and claws slashed through warm flesh. The cries of the dying soldiers filled his beast with satisfaction.

Time moved too slowly as he fought his way to Zamira. Akia took off at a dead run heading straight for the wall below Daemon's platform. He jumped using the soldiers in front of him as a launching pad to send himself half way up the wall. Unconcerned about the pain, he buried his claws into the stone and scaled it by sheer will.

Akia howled in frustration to find the area devoid of any of the members of Daemon's entourage. Where could they have taken her? His beast raised his nose to the air and found that faint floral scent that he recognized as uniquely Zamira's.

Akia crouched down on all fours and closed his eyes. His heightened sense of smell finally gave him a direction to follow and he sprang into action.

Mid-leap he was knocked to the ground by his phased brother. Akia the man was buried so deeply behind the instincts of the beast that he didn't recognize the worry in his brother's face at his actions. All the beast recognized was another obstacle to overcome before he could retrieve his mate.

Akia snarled and rolled into a fighting stance.

Akia, please…

Banji tried to touch his brother's mind but all he found was rage and the beginnings of despair. It was as if Akia had gone mad.

"Don't make me do this, brother."

Akia circled Banji with a deep rumbling growl. Then he burst into action. Claws slashing in rapid succession. If Banji hadn't spent the majority of his life sparing with his brother he would have been killed almost instantly.

Banji was at a disadvantage. He wasn't trying to kill Akia; but Akia seemed to be trying to kill him. Banji knew that Akia would luck into a deadly strike if they remained facing each other for too long. Akia always had been better at hand-to-hand combat, even if at one time he preferred to work as a sniper. Banji's only hope was to get close and personal where his skill at grappling out matched his brother's. Getting that close was a gamble with an enraged phased.

Banji fought and observed, finding the rhythm of movement of this more fierce Akia. Slowly a pattern was starting to emerge. To the casual observer, Akia's attacks seemed almost random; however, Banji saw that he was concentrating his blows to the left side…Banji's weaker side.

Banji became distracted when his men rappelled down from the walk way above the arena. Banji shook his head to warn them away from interfering, but in that brief moment Akia landed a blow. Claws ripped across Banji's ribs before he could move out of their reach.

Banji knew that Akia would press the advantage and attack that weakened area again, so he deliberately left himself open. When Akia lunged for him he used his brother's momentum and turned with the attack until both men were on the ground.

Here Banji had always bested his brother, but he had never dealt with Akia's drug-enhanced strength Akia before. Banji knew he wasn't going to be able to wear his brother down because his brother didn't even seem winded while Banji's muscles trembled with exertion.

He twisted his limbs around Akia, tangling legs and pinning arms painfully behind his brother's back. It wasn't a position he had strength to hold for long, but it did allow him to free up one hand so he could reach into his uniform and grab the sedative that all of Kavi's operatives carried on them for emergencies.

Banji wasn't gentle with its administration. He jabbed the device into Akia's neck and released the drug. Akia continued to struggle but his movements became sluggish until they stopped altogether. Banji checked to make sure his brother was well and truly unconscious before unwinding himself from his brother's limbs and standing up.

"I'm sorry, Akia," Banji whispered.

One of the other men come over and looked down at the phased and unconscious form of Akia.

"Why hasn't he unphased?"

"I don't know. We will figure it out later." Banji ran a hand through his sweaty hair. "For now let's just get him home."

*****

Banji sat next to the prone body of Akia. Everyone was relieved when he finally unphased about halfway back to the rendezvous point. A man should unphase as soon as he lost consciousness. The fact that Akia didn't just wasn't normal and punctuated the fact that they had no idea what all he had been through in the last year.

Part of Banji felt guilty because this past year had been one of the best of his life while his brother suffered. But even if it made him a selfish man, he couldn't regret Maria and their children. She and the twins were a gift from the gods.

Akia finally began to stir, which was good timing as their transport was scheduled to arrive any minute. Banji moved closer to help his brother sit up. He knew from experience that the drug could leave a person dizzy and queasy.

"Zamira!" Akia shot up to a sitting position before falling back onto the pallet with a groan. He rolled over and glared at Banji. "Where is Zamira?"

Banji handed his brother a canteen of water. "I don't even know who Zamira is."

"My mate…she is my mate." Akia rubbed his temple. "I remember fighting my way to her in Daemon's platform at the arena. There were soldiers everywhere, but I cut through them easily. But someone stopped me…You!"

Banji held up his hands and eyed his brother nervously as fur rippled across Akia's skin.

"I swear I thought you had gone crazy or something. That's why I knocked you out."

"How could you keep me from my mate?" Akia bellowed.

The men sent to rescue Akia began to gather at the commotion, a few with weapons drawn. They had all witnessed Akia's loss of control earlier. In fact, a couple had suggested keeping Akia sedated until they were able to get him to a mental health facility on Vukas. Banji had refused trusting that his brother would never actually harm him. That trust was looking a little thin in light of this new information.

"Because I didn't know you had a mate!" Banji

matched Akia for volume. "You forgot to inform me of such an important detail. The five hells, Akia, if I had known you had a mate I would have made sure she was rescued tonight too."

"How could I forget to tell you about Zamira? She is everything to me. Without her the beast wins." Akia choked on the last few words as he fought to keep his tears at bay.

Banji kneeled down by his brother and laid a hand on his shoulder. "We had two truncated half-assed conversations before all hell broke loose. None of us considered that you might find something so important while imprisoned." Banji plopped down next to his brother and waved off the other warriors. "Which was stupid of me especially considering I found my own mate in a prison cell."

"How is Maria doing?"

Banji and Akia spent a little while catching up. Akia smiled for the first time in Banji's presence when he found out he was an uncle to a niece and nephew. Akia didn't talk much about his time as a gladiator slave, but the taciturn man waxed poetic about the absent Zamira. Banji would be forever grateful to her for saving his brother's sanity.

It wasn't long before Banji's communicator went off informing him that their transport was in orbit.

"Time to go, brother." Banji stood brushing the

dust from his pants.

"Tell Maria I said hello and I wish you both happiness." Akia stood and attempted to embrace his brother.

"You're coming with us. A squadron of the galactic fleet is orbiting the planet. The Admiral Batu is heading up the offensive. This whole place will soon be a war zone, that city being the epicenter of it all. We'll come back with a proper team and plan to rescue Zamira and free the rest of this planets inhabitants."

"I understand that you need to get back to your mate and offspring, Banji but I am not leaving this planet without *my* mate. The fact that she is my mate is reason enough that I wouldn't leave her behind but she is powerful in her own right. I have studied Daemon for the last year. I know how he thinks. She will only survive long enough to draw me out. If he finds out I left the planet he will kill her because it is the strategic move."

"If that is true you will be walking into a trap."

"Which is why I want you to get on that ship and go back to Maria. You have done enough getting me out of that prison. I will do the rest."

Banji pulled at his hair and kicked a stone that laid near his foot, "*Frexing* five hells! Maria, not to mention Megan, would kick my ass if I left you behind alone."

"I'm not letting you walk into what could very well be a suicide mission." Akia grabbed his brother's face and made him look him in the eyes. "You have a family. You have to be there for them. Damn the moons, without Zamira I am nothing. I would turn into a monster to be feared by all because she is my only reason for living. Can't you understand that?"

Before Banji could respond the young soldier, Jax, emerged from a nearby tree.

"I'll stay and help him," Jax stated standing tall.

Banji and Akia both gave the young whelp the 'are you kidding?' look.

"I might not be a great warrior, but I have worked all over this city. I know most likely where Lord Daemon will be and I know how to move around without being noticed. When your officers are encouraged to be sadistic bastards it's a good skill to have."

Akia nodded and his brother, Banji, sighed. "You know there was a time when you were the reasonable one and I was the one always getting into trouble." Banji pulled at his hair and groaned. "Fine. I'll go back to Reijo and tell him what is going on here. You are taking a communicator and pulling rank whether you want to or not. There is a battalion that will remain here until the full offensive begins." He grabbed Akia by the shirt and shook him. "Use them. You better survive this mess or I am going to kill you. Understand?"

CHAPTER NINETEEN

Jax and Akia crouched behind some building debris. The city had devolved into chaos. The fighters flew through the air attacking pockets of Tanis soldiers. Buildings were blown apart. As with any war there were civilian casualties.

Akia hardened his heart against the sight of the body of a young girl staring at him with sightless eyes. Young Jax's heart wasn't so easily buried and Akia had to pull him away before they wasted time trying to bury those they could no longer help. He vowed to Jax and the spirit of that girl that when Zamira was safe he would do everything in his power to restore peace to Ludus Prime.

They were halfway through the city when they spotted a group of Tanis soldiers assaulting three of the native women. Without strong leadership, the Tanis acted like a gang of thugs rather than warriors. The strategic thing to do for their mission would be to use the unfortunate women's experience as a distraction to make it through enemy lines undetected. But Akia knew that now that Jax had chosen to stand his moral ground instead of following his former clan's leadership that he wouldn't be able to walk past such a scene. And the truth was Akia didn't want to walk past it either. With a few whispered words and hand signals Jax nodded that he understood the plan.

Akia phased and launched himself at the soldiers. He knocked the one who had a woman pinned to the ground off of her. Akia had him gutted before they even hit the ground. He rolled and stood using the soldier's body as a shield to absorb the hits from the energy weapons of the remaining soldiers. With a roar, Akia threw away the body of the dead soldier, when the poorly trained Tanis had emptied the energy from their weapons and had to wait for them to recharge.

A few of the soldiers tried to flee only to be stopped by Jax, who judiciously shot them down without wasting ammunition. The rest pulled their energy blades from their belts and activated them to sword length.

Akia smiled his feral smile and adjusted his fighting stance, a panting laugh escaped through his fangs as he smelled their fear. He was their worst nightmare, the uncaged Vukasin Beast. They stood there frozen in time for a moment before Akia launched into his deadly dance.

He slashed through the soldiers with tooth and claw. They didn't have time for him to play with his prey so his strikes were almost surgical in their precision. Akia struck blow to each man to kill him as quickly as possible. His skill was such that even when one of the soldiers pulled one of the women in front of his as a shield, the only thing to touch the woman was the blood of her enemy.

In short order Akia stood at the center of a bloody circle of dead. Jax stared at him in equal measures of admiration and horror. The women huddled together in a terrified mass, clinging to each other as if that would somehow keep them safe.

The women screamed when Akia forced himself to unphase. The beast was strong in him today because he was going after his mate. If it wasn't for the fact that Akia knew he would have a better chance of getting to Zamira in his unphased form, he would have stayed the beast until her music could sooth him. As it was his unphasing was a slow and difficult process. He remained in the grotesque in-between period much longer than any Vukasin before.

When he finally returned to the man, Akia approached the women only to have them cringe away from him in fear despite the fact that he had just saved them. He tried not to let the reaction hurt him but it made him feel like he had truly become a monster.

Jax rushed over to the women when Akia turned away. He could tell their fear of Akia hurt him. Akia's back was turned and he didn't see the women cringe in fear when Jax approached. They didn't fear Akia specifically, they feared all Vukasin men and not without just cause.

"Hurry. Leave the city if you can. It isn't safe here." Jax spoke softly to the women but his tone conveyed the urgency of his statement. A building near them rocked the ground with an explosion, punctuating the need to hurry.

The woman holding the other two protectively nodded. Without a word she grabbed the hands of her companions and they ran off down the street heading for the jungle that surrounded the city.

Jax stood up and dusted himself off once they made it out of his sight. He jogged to catch up to Akia.

"You know it wasn't just you."

"What?" Akia asked in confusion.

"The women. They weren't just scared of you. They were scared of me too."

Akia smiled a sad smile and clapped Jax on the back as they made their way toward the other end of the city. "You're a good man, Jax."

"Even if I am a Tanis."

Akia's laugh sounded rough and gravelly from disuse. "Even if you are a Tanis."

CHAPTER TWENTY

Fighters swarmed overhead. The sky was filled with fire from the energy weapons. The building they were targeting remained untouched. Part of Akia was relieved. If Zamira was truly in that building, at least she was safe from the attacking fleet for the time being.

Akia studied the compound they were trying to enter. Jax said that it had been the royal palace before the Tanis invasion. After Daemon had executed the entire royal household on Bel's orders, he decided it was the best place for him to set up his own little empire. Daemon had had the place refurbished and rebuilt as his fortress. When all of the systems were activated it was almost impenetrable. Which was their current problem.

It made sense for Daemon to retreat here if he was under attack. Thankfully his defenses acted as much as a prison as it did a defense.

"Are you sure you can get us in?" Akia asked.

Jax sighed. "For the third time, yes I am sure."

"Sorry, I just don't see how you can get us in if the Imperial fleet can't get through their defenses."

"Because we aren't going through their defenses."

Jax motioned for Akia to follow him. They worked their way through the thick jungle surrounding the compound. In the distance Akia heard a haunting sound. It was almost like hundreds of women singing a mournful song, except it had no words just tones. It made Akia stop and turn his head to try and capture more of the song, as if he could divine its meaning if he heard more.

"That is the air organ. Evidently sound is considered sacred to the people here on Ludus Prime. Supposedly the song will change if something bad is about to happen. Probably explains why it always sounded like it was crying to me," Jax explained to Akia.

"You seem to know quite a bit about the people here."

Jax shrugged, "You learn a lot of things when you treat people with respect. I was a lowly foot soldier. I did the menial jobs just like the natives forced into servitude here. I wasn't better than them just because I was Vukasin."

"Of course not."

"You would be surprised how many of the men here thought they were superior just because they were Vukasin. Then add on top of that the belief that they were better than most Vukasin just because they were Tanis. It bred a lot of ugliness, especially towards the natives."

Akia stopped and turned towards Jax. "But you treated them differently."

"I treated them with respect, not differently. Everyone deserves respect until they show you otherwise."

"You are a rather wise man for one so young."

"I had good examples growing up." Jax turned back to hack through the jungle with his energy blade, getting lost in his memories. "Our village was very remote. It edged the desert and the mountains that divided the Tanis territory from the Torolf on the other side of the mountain. Our side of the mountain was much harsher than the Torolf side, but it still received more rainwater than anywhere else in the Tanis territory. We had to work twice as hard for half the crop, but we still were able to make things grow and we were proud of what we could do. Being so far away made it pretty much impossible to send the few whelps we had to a warrior's den, so I grew up with my family. They were good men." Jax paused, "I'm probably the last of them."

"I'm sure they would be proud of the man you have become."

Jax's smile was a little sad. "I hope so…Anyway, they taught me that you give respect to everyone until they prove they are not worthy of that respect."

"Let's stop here and rest." Akia sat on a fallen tree and pulled a canteen from the pack he carried. He rifled through the supplies. "It looks like we have dehydrated nutrient bars, nutrient bars, and…oh look a nutrient bar."

Jax smiled but didn't laugh as Akia handed him a nutrient bar and a canteen of water. Akia knew that remembering better times could leave you melancholy and didn't push the young man. Instead he munched on the tough and tasteless survival food.

"So where exactly are we going?"

"When I first got here I was sent to help and supervise the cleaning crews in Daemon's fortress. Being the new guy, they of course assigned me to the dungeon duty. The dungeons there were rarely, if ever, used because if Daemon wanted to torture or punish someone he just sent them to the arena. But the places still needed to be kept clean to keep the vermin out. Daemon actually has a big phobia about critters crawling on him in his sleep. With the city and his fortress surrounded by jungle it was an ongoing battle to keep small creatures out."

"How did you find out about the phobia?"

Jax laughed, "One night a small, harmless lizard got into his suite of rooms and he evidently woke up with the thing on his face. The startled lizard scurried off him and hid of course, but he mobilized an entire unit to search his suite until the poor lizard was found and dispatched."

"So what does being in the dungeons have to do with where you are leading me? I mean my instincts tell me I can trust you but the truth is you could be leading me into a trap."

Jax closed his canteen and handed it back to Akia to put away into the survival pack. "You're right. I could be, but I'm not. I was the only Tanis soldier down in the dungeons. The rest of the workers were natives, a mix of mostly women with the odd male. They fully expected me to beat and abuse them, so it came as a shock when I jumped in to help finish the various tasks. They were the ones who showed me where we are going. If any of them are still there, they will help us find Zamira as well."

The men packed up their meager meal and continued their trek through the jungle. The sounds of the fighters attacking the palace were drowned out by the music of the air organ. Soon the pair broke free of the jungle to overlook a deep gorge. It was here that the air organ had been carved from the stone of the cliffs on either side of the gorge. At the bottom of the gorge was a fast moving river.

"I hope the Tiaret training is as good as they say it is. We have to rappel down to the riverside from here."

Akia had already pulled rope from their survival pack and was tying his seat with an expert hand. "Watch and learn, whelp." He threw a length of rope at Jax.

Jax quickly secured the ropes at the top of the cliff. Both him and Akia tested their knots and seats. They leaned out over the gorge.

"Race you to the bottom, old man," Jax challenged before launching himself into the air.

CHAPTER TWENTY-ONE

The sound of the air organ was deafening at the bottom of the gorge. The whole landscape seemed to act like an echo chamber amplifying the sound exponentially. Akia found his voice disappeared in the roaring of the air organ. He could well imagine that to the native people the noise appeared like an angry god, challenging all who dared to enter.

Akia tensed when Jax placed a hand on his

shoulder. Using hand signals, Jax made Akia understand that he needed to follow. They followed a treacherous trail along the river's edge. The water line on the rock wall next to them showed that the trail would disappear during a heavy rain as the water level would rise above it.

Akia nearly fell as his foot slipped on the damp rock. The roaring of the air organ made his head pound. He closed his eyes for a moment trying to relieve the ache. When he opened them he realized that Jax was no longer on the trail in front of him. He moved forward cautiously while trying to watch the roaring water of the river racing ahead of him. Did Jax slip and fall off the tight trail into the river? He couldn't see Jax, but the current was so strong it could have washed him far down stream in a moment. Akia called for Jax even though his voice couldn't be heard over the angry sound of the air organ.

Suddenly a hand grabbed Akia, pulling him into an entrance to a cave that was hidden behind the jungle vine climbing the cliff wall. One moment he was deafened by sacred noise and the next…silence. He only heard the pounding of his heart. The entire effect was disorienting.

"Give it a moment and the pounding in your head will pass," Jax whispered.

"You sound as if this isn't the first time you have traveled this path," Akia answered equally as quiet.

Jax shrugged, "One of the native women gave birth to a daughter while she worked in the dungeons. She had been raped by one of the Tanis soldiers. She begged me to take the child out before Daemon discovered it. He was known to kill any child he deemed worthless, though those that he allowed to survive often fared even worse. You see, the soldiers weren't kept track of as closely as the slaves. After I agreed the natives showed me this place."

"Do you know what happened to the whelp?"

"I took her to an old woman at the edge of the city. That was the last I saw of her. Supposedly the woman sneaks the children out of the city when she can and takes them to the rural communities hidden in the jungles. Daemon doesn't have as much control in those areas and many communities remain hidden according to the natives."

Akia filed that information away for later. It was good to know that their might be others not under Daemon's control.

Jax raised his finger to his lips indicating the need for silence. Then Akia heard it. The voice was distorted and echoed through the chamber.

"I swear to you I heard voices. Maybe this place really is haunted by the spirits of the dead, like the natives say." Vukasin voices drifted down the hall.

"Superstitious dragon-spider shit. Hurry up and finish the inventory. It's my turn with the new girl and I refuse to lose my chance to dip my dick because you are scared," another voice said.

Akia and Jax slowly and silently made their way towards the voices. The distance was surprisingly far considering they could distinctly make out the guards' conversation. They emerged into the lower bowels of the dungeon behind a series of shelves. The opening was narrow and angled in such a way that unless you knew it was there you probably wouldn't notice it along the stone wall. It wasn't made for large Vukasin frames and for a moment Akia panicked because he thought he wouldn't be able to get through. This path was obviously meant for the more delicate native population.

Holding his breath and sucking in his gut as far as it would go, allowed Akia to just barely squeeze through. He found Jax kneeling behind crates watching the two guards in the room. From the look on his face, Akia knew that Jax wanted to save this "new girl" from the attentions of the Tanis. Turning his eyes towards the two men, he could understand why. Both were abnormally large and reeked of the strength-enhancing drugs the Tanis liked to pump into their foot soldiers. Akia knew from personal experience that those drugs also increased aggression and brutality. At some point those men if they lived would become the deformed phased and end up as fodder for the arena.

Logically, Akia knew they should leave the men to their business so as not to alert anyone to their presence, but the look on Jax's face told him that he wouldn't allow those men to leave alive. Sighing in resignation, Akia moved closer to his targets. He could take down one of them silently, but the other would have a chance to sound the alarm. Akia couldn't do it alone.

Jax moved next to Akia. With hand signals he said he would take the man on the left, leaving the larger of the two to Akia. Akia tried to convey that they needed to kill quickly and silently. Jax nodded and Akia hoped the young man truly understood.

Akia held up three fingers and used them to count down. When the count ended both men burst from their hiding place. Akia wrenched his target's head, snapping his neck before he could make a sound. Jax used an energy blade which he sunk into the base of his target's skull severing the spine and vocal cords at the same time. The only sound was both bodies thumping on the floor, but the air was filled with the smell of cauterized flesh. Jax had upped the burn of the energy blade to prevent blood from spilling. Akia was impressed that Jax had considered the need to prevent blood from leaving a trail.

The pair stashed the bodies within a couple of the storage crates filled with weaponry. They had stumbled upon Daemon's armory. Akia and Jax armed themselves with several different weapons.

Akia allowed Jax to take point since he knew the way around the palace compound. He led them to a corridor the next level up. Numerous voices floated down the hallway and Akia tensed for a fight. Instead of turning away from the voices Jax headed straight for them. Akia worried that what was supposed to be a rescue mission had turned into a revenge vendetta for Jax. But he had no way of knowing where Zamira might be and Jax was his only map. So he followed him, but kept his finger on the trigger of the stunner he pulled from the armory.

The voices seemed to mostly come from a room halfway down the hall. Jax peeked in and then to Akia's horror walked straight into the room. Akia raised his weapon and filled the doorway prepared to fire on the enemy only to find Jax hugging a tiny native woman who gasped when she saw Akia. Jax immediately moved to place his body in the line of fire but relaxed when he saw Akia.

"Gia, allow me to introduce the mate of High Priestess Zamira."

The woman, Gia, moved to examine Akia. Upon closer inspection it was clear that Gia was much older than he had first thought. Though her hair was still the dark black of the native people with only a few streaks of silver, her face held lines of age and her eyes held a wisdom that only the old seemed to carry. Akia looked into her eyes and she didn't turn away like most did from his predatory gaze. He knew she could see the beast below the surface.

He evidently passed some sort of test because Gia nodded and stated, "He will do."

"Gia was once an elder of the city. She didn't wield the same power as the priestesses of Ti'lak, but she has her own goddess-given gifts." Jax turned to the woman and bowed, "Can you help us, Gia?"

Gia smiled at Jax and patted his cheek. "You were always such a respectful boy. Of course I will help. With the royal family gone, only the High Priestess can hold our society together." Gia took Akia's hand. "Do you understand your role, young man?"

Akia's beast was getting impatient at the delays. "I am her mate," he growled.

Gia frowned, "That is what you need from her, boy. Do you know what she needs from you?"

Akia thought about the beautiful, serene Zamira. She was everything he was not. She would never use her power, no matter how great, to harm another. She was kind and generous; but her kindness made her vulnerable. She needed someone to deal with the ugliness of life; to defend her from the evils of the universe. There couldn't be light without darkness.

"I am her shield, her tooth, and claw." Akia stood straighter as he made his declaration. "I will protect and defend my mate. I will hunt down and destroy those who threaten my mate. I am her beast and I will guard her."

Gia's wrinkled face broke into a smile. "I knew you would do. Our world has changed and it will change much more in the near future. I foresaw that our two worlds will forever be connected. We need you, Zamira needs you. Without you, she cannot lead our people to a place where we can prosper. And I have a feeling that your world needs us as much as we now need you."

"No offense, Elder Gia," Akia growled through clenched teeth. The beast was ready to hunt and it was taking all of his will to keep control. "But we can worry about the fate of the world *after* I save Zamira."

"Quite right." Gia walked over to a large pile of laundry and threw a uniform at Akia similar to the one that Jax was wearing. "Put this on. We can't do much about your face, but the soldiers here are used to seeing new faces on a regular basis. Perhaps it will be enough."

Aka quickly changed into the Tanis uniform. Wearing Bel's colors made his skin crawl but he would do what was necessary to get his mate to safety.

"Zamira is being kept in the east wing tower. That is Daemon's private domain. Once you get to the east wing soldiers are rare, so you won't be able to hide in the masses like you can in the rest of the palace. I'll send word to other trusted slaves. Trust only those that speak of the 'holy song.' That is how you will know whom to trust."

"I would think that all of the natives would want to help us." Jax showed his youth and naivety in that moment.

"There are good and bad people in any community, young Jax. There are also those who will follow power no matter how dark and corrupt." Gia imparted the life lesson to Jax, it was now up to him whether he learned from it now or learned it later the hard way.

Gia whistled a three-note tune and a native man appeared. It was the first time Akia had seen one of the native men. They were larger and more muscular than the native women, but were still much smaller than a Vukasin male.

The man's eyes widened at the sight of two Vukasin men in Tanis uniforms. But he didn't back down even though Akia could smell his fear. Akia respected the man's bravery. The man bowed to Elder Gia.

"You have need of me, Elder?"

"Rolo, these men are here for the High Priestess."

Akia observed the native man change his stance as if preparing to fight.

"What need have you of the Priestess?" his gruff voice questioned.

Akia was fairly certain that had it not been Elder Gia who had summoned him, the man would have attacked first and asked questions later. It was good to know that there were still people of action within the native population. It would make rebuilding their world easier.

"She is my mate," Akia growled.

Rolo squared off to Akia despite the scent of fear rolling off him in waves. Akia understood but he didn't have time to appease the prejudice of every native they met. Fur rippled across Akia's skin, as a deep warning rumbled in his chest.

Elder Gia laid a hand on both men's arms. She watched Rolo with wise eyes.

"Elder, no…you do not know this man. I saw one of his fights in the arena." Rolo looked Akia in the eye. "Yes, I know who you are." Rolo turned pleading eyes to the Elder. "Even his own people called him The Beast."

"Then you know what I am capable of," Akia growled.

"Which is exactly why I will not hand our Priestess over to you. What makes you think that you are worthy of her?"

"I'm not worthy of her."

Akia's declaration shocked the man into silence.

"I will never be worthy; but no man will love her as deeply as I do. She is my world, my reason to exist. I will never betray her."

Rolo stared at Akia for a long time before doing an about face.

"Follow me," Rolo said in a low gruff voice.

*****

Akia and Jax found themselves being led by torch light through windowless stone tunnels. The passageway wasn't made for the large Vukasin men and often Akia had to stoop to keep from hitting his head.

After many minutes of silence Rolo finally spoke. "I know and trust Jax to help us because he has helped us before, but how do I know that I can trust you to help us?"

"You can't. I have no loyalty to you," Akia replied.

"Yet you expect me to hand over our Priestess to

you." Rolo shook his head. "Let's assume that I lead you to the Priestess and you manage to escape with her. What will you do afterwards?"

Akia shrugged as he turned sideways to make it through a narrow doorway. "That will be Zamira's choice. I will follow where she goes."

"So you won't take her away from Ludus Prime?"

"It is her choice. If she chooses to leave, then we will leave."

"She won't abandon her people," Rolo declared with conviction.

Akia said nothing more, it wasn't necessary. He had only told the truth. While he empathized with the people of Ludus Prime, he was Zamira's beast, not theirs. In the end if he had to choose he would always choose her.

Rolo opened a large wooden door and waved Jax and Akia into a cavernous rotunda lit by a multitude of torches. Numerous natives - both men and women- milled about the room. Scattered around the outer ring were several stations filled with different types of weaponry. Akia could tell that much of the weaponry was projectile based instead of energy based. A few Vukasin weapons were scattered among the hodgepodge armory.

"Gentlemen, welcome to the resistance."

CHAPTER TWENTY-TWO

Zamira paced her gilded cage. The only reason she hadn't been placed in the dank dungeon was because Daemon was certain that Akia would come for her.

Part of her wanted that to be true. The idea of dying at Daemon's hands frightened her because she felt it in her soul that he would not make it an easy death. The other part of her prayed to Ti'lak that Akia had escaped this planet with his brother.

Dust rained down from the rafters. The fighters had been attacking steadily since their arrival. So far Daemon's energy shields were holding, but Zamira wondered just how much more bombardment they would be able to take. Eventually they would fail and if the fighters continued their onslaught at this pace, the old royal palace would be reduced to rubble. If it wasn't for the hundreds of innocent lives confined to the palace, Zamira almost wished it would be destroyed. The royal family had been destroyed and Daemon had tainted its history with his presence.

Another blast landed on the shield directly overhead knocking Zamira to the ground. She crawled to the bed and sprawled across it. With the steady stream of attacks Daemon had locked her in this room within his private wing. She knew he planned on violating her before he killed her. He had laid out those plans when he dragged her away from both the arena and Akia. The attacks on his stronghold had kept him away from her. *I should be thankful for small miracles.*

For the first time since the Tanis invaded her world, Zamira felt truly hopeless. She rolled over to her side while tears tracked down her face.

"Great Goddess…why have your forsaken us?" Zamira cried to the empty room.

She had tried to live her life according to the teachings passed down generation after generation.

Her voice held the capacity to enslave and kill, but she chose to use it to guide and comfort. Had she been wrong? Had the goddess gifted her with such a powerful gift because she was supposed to use it as a weapon to protect her people?

Zamira buried her face into the fancy bedding and sobbed. She wondered if all of this was somehow her fault. If she had used her gift at the beginning to control the outsiders…would it have changed anything?

A long buried memory bubbled to the surface of her mind. She had been barely a woman outside of childhood. Her voice had matured into its full power. She had been playing at the edge of the temple grounds where the jungle started. She had been experimenting with the power of her voice, using it to control a small flock of colorful birds. She thought it was amazing to direct their movements and flight just by changing the tone of the notes she sang. She choreographed an entire aerial dance. She was lost in her own power when a temple guard who had been sent to search for her startled Zamira. In her fright she reached a crescendo and squealed up the scale rapidly changing her notes, but she hadn't shut off her power and control of the birds. Suddenly the entire flock fell to the ground either stone dead or in the final twitches before expiring. That was the day she learned that she could stop a heart and kill with the power of her voice. She had cried for days thinking she was a monster. The high priestess became even more strict, teaching Zamira absolute control. She assured Zamira that the goddess didn't hand out gifts randomly, so there must be a reason she was given such a power. All of that brought Zamira back to wondering if she had made a mistake by not using herself as a weapon, even though she still mourned for those beautiful birds years later. How much more would the soul of a man or woman weigh on her own?

Music suddenly filled Zamira's mind and she sang. She sang a dirge for those who were lost. She sang about what might have been. The music allowed her to work through the thoughts that raced through her mind. Somewhere in the song Zamira found herself again. The mournful melody changed to a song of rising hope and her heart lifted. She was alive. Akia was alive. As long as there was life, there was hope.

Zamira closed her eyes as the blasts from the fighters beat a bass rhythm outside. As she drifted off to sleep another song filled her mind: a call to arms. If she managed to live through this she knew that she would use her power. Not as a weapon, at least not directly, but as a unifying force. She would rally her people like the battle queens of old. Once they expelled their enemies, they would rebuild a changing world.

It was a powerful song with an equally powerful vision. But it wasn't time to sing it just yet.

CHAPTER TWENTY-THREE

"Why are we wasting time here?" Akia cornered Rolo.

They had spent two nights among the rebels. His beast was clawing at his mind that they needed their mate. Logically Akia knew that rushing in would be a mistake, but he was quickly getting to the point that the beast's need to get to its mate would override the logic of the man who wanted to make sure both of them were alive at the end of this.

Rolo was still decidedly uncomfortable around Akia, in fact most of the men were. Oddly enough the native women seemed more at ease once it was discovered that his loyalty was for Zamira alone.

"Patience. You may be here to only rescue our priestess, but the rest of us are trying to rescue our entire world," Rolo replied.

Akia ran his hand through his hair and pulled trying to get his beast to settle. "I know. But she is so close and I have this feeling that if we don't get to her soon it will be too late."

Akia sank down on the floor and leaned against a crate of weapons, banging his head against the rough wood.

"Rolo, I know you don't know me and I know that you fear me..." Akia's eyes stared off at the ceiling but he wasn't seeing the stone, he was seeing Zamira's beautiful face. She appeared so delicate. He could see her soft, pale olive skin surrounding huge amethyst eyes with sparks of gold. He had never seen such unique eyes before. Her long hair cascaded down her back like a midnight water fall. Her smile rivaled the sun in his eyes and her voice was his salvation.

"Yes?" Rolo prompted Akia to continue.

Akia closed his eyes locking the memory of Zamira away before turning earnest eyes to Rolo. "I must ask a boon of you. It is something that I cannot ask of young Jax."

Rolo slid to the ground to sit across from Akia intrigued by what this powerful man would ask of him. He would be lying if he said he didn't still have a healthy dose of fear of the Vukasin Beast, but over the last couple of days he had also come to respect the man as well. Akia was impressive in his battle strategy. He helped them plan a course of action that might keep this attack from being a suicide mission. He gave them communication frequencies to the Imperial ships attacking the palace from above and told them to use his name. Akia didn't have to do any of that if his only goal was saving the high priestess, but he did so because he knew her people were important to her.

"What would you ask of me?" Rolo questioned.

"If, the gods forbid, we are too late and Zamira is no more, you must kill me. Otherwise I will become the monster everyone fears me to be. As a Vukasin, Jax would be hard pressed to take me out because of my reputation and connections to our royal house. Plus, he is young and kind hearted, forcing him to kill someone he views as a friend would take away some of the idealism that this universe needs to become a better place."

Rolo leaned back against his own crate and gave a gruff chuckle. "You are much different than I thought you would be. It would have been easier to kill you when I thought you were just a beast who happened to be loyal to the priestess. It is much more difficult to kill someone you know to be a good man."

Akia gave a rueful smile. "If it makes you feel any better, without Zamira I would no longer be a good man."

"You truly love her don't you?"

"She is my everything."

Rolo stood up and held his hand out to Akia. "Well then I guess we have to make sure that you both survive."

Akia took Rolo's hand and allowed the man to help him up. They were about to make their way to the rest of the rebel forces when a messenger arrived and everyone burst into action.

Akia and Rolo looked at each other and without a word took off at a jog to find out what had suddenly changed.

*****

"Ground forces have surrounded the energy shield of the palace. They are obviously other Vukasins but their uniforms are different from the Tanis," one of the rebels reported.

"That would be the imperial forces. Batu, the man leading them, is from my clan. He is an honorable man. If you can get messages in my name to him he will help you," Akia said, looking at the readout showing where the rebels had found troops. Batu was settling in for a long siege since his fighters hadn't been able to break through the energy shield surrounding the palace. "Did we locate where their shield generators are?"

"We have three possible locations. We cannot confirm since slaves are forbidden from entering those areas," one of the warrior women stated.

"We could attack all three simultaneously," Jax said.

"We don't have enough manpower to successfully do that," Rolo added.

Akia thought for a moment. "Is the gorge where the air organ is the only way to get around the energy shield?"

Rolo thought for a moment. "There is a similar subterranean exit on the other side of the palace as well. They were old escape routes for the royal family that no one but those trusted by the royal family knew about. We discovered the gorge exit first because the Vukasins complained about the sound, so they left that area alone allowing us to work without supervision. Also, they didn't think that there was anything below the dungeon area."

"Get a couple of your fastest runners. I will compose a message for the *kijanis* of the troops surrounding us. With their added manpower we can hit all three locations. This ends tonight." Akia eyed each rebel until they nodded their agreement.

CHAPTER TWENTY-FOUR

"Wake up, you little whore!" Daemon yelled.

Zamira was jerked out of bed and thrown to the floor. The sun had set outside and the room was plunged into shadows. She had slept for hours. She had been so exhausted that she hadn't heard Daemon enter the room. That was a mistake she now regretted as the man loomed over her.

The deep shadows gave Daemon a demonic look.

His outer appearance finally reflected his inner character. His eyes held a madness that Zamira had never seen before. He was cruel before but his actions always seemed deliberate. Now he seemed almost frantic in his rage.

"You ruined everything!" Spittle landed on Zamira's face as Daemon yelled at her. "We could have ruled this world if you had just sung for me." Daemon grabbed her arm and hauled her off the floor. His fingers gripped her so hard that she was afraid he would break bone. "But you had to sing for him! Now Ivalio has sent their dogs to my door."

Daemon dragged her to the window. Zamira could see an army camped just outside the perimeter of the energy shield.

"I know you have the power to control even a force of this size. You proved that that day in the arena. One last time, you will sing for me."

Zamira struggled against Daemon's implacable grip. "No, I will not sing for you."

"Then I have no use for you." Daemon carried her back to the bed and threw her down. "But I will have a little fun before I dispose of you."

Zamira tried to run, but Daemon used his weight and strength to pin her down. He grabbed one hand and buckled her into restraints attached to the corner of the massive bed. Zamira hadn't noticed them when she had collapsed on the bed to rest. That was a mistake. She should have searched the room for something useful instead of fretting about things she could no longer change.

With one hand secured Daemon moved to her other hand. She fought and kicked until he had all four limbs restrained. He the cinched up the ropes until she was spread-eagle and unable to move no matter how much she struggled. She was at his mercy.

Daemon moved away from the bed and stared down at her with a feral grin. He watched her, feeding off of her fear. Her heart felt like it was going to beat out of her chest; her eyes darted frantically around the room hoping for some sort of miracle to materialize. She started to panic and Daemon's eyes lit up with glee. It was then that her rational mind started to kick back in. She knew that she would live longer if she let her terror show because he would want to toy with her. She wondered whether it was worth going through the torture he planned for a few minutes or hours more of life.

Suddenly a love song whispered through her mind and she knew Akia was somewhere near. It may have been only wishful thinking but it spurred her will to survive. She had to survive for her people, for herself…but mostly for him. Akia needed her and she, by the goddess, needed him to.

Her terrified eyes turned to defiance as she glared at Daemon.

"Ah, there is the proud priestess," Daemon hiss. "I'm going to enjoy breaking you."

Daemon turned to the cabinet behind him and opened it. Zamira craned her neck to see what he was doing as he whistled cheerfully to himself. Of course Zamira had heard the rumors of Daemon's predilections. She had seen the poor battered women after they had been sent to him. She knew about the women and even the odd male, who was never seen again after they went to 'service' Lord Daemon.

The cabinet opened to display Daemon's toys. An assortment of whips, knives, and items she had no idea what they were for; but she seriously doubted she wanted to find out. Daemon dithered back and forth before choosing a short narrow whip.

Daemon turned to her and raised his hand, cracking the whip across her stomach. The slight strip of leather ripped through the material of her simple dress, exposing her skin and leaving a stinging red welt across her midsection. Daemon demonstrated his skill with the whip when the next blow landed in exactly the same position opening her skin

Zamira couldn't contain the cry of pain as blood welled up across the injury. Please, goddess, let Akia get here soon.

Daemon raised his hand again only to be knocked to the ground when the entire palace shook from an explosion. Daemon ran to the window and let out a string of curses when another explosion rocked the ground. This blast was much closer and caused dust and stone to rain down from the walls and ceiling above.

For a moment Zamira held out hope that Daemon would forget about her among this new development. But she wasn't so lucky.

Daemon turned to her and stalked to the bed. The mattress sunk as his weight settled beside her. He caressed her face and Zamira recoiled at his touch. He smiled at her obvious disgust.

"Well, little song bird, it seems that my play time has been cut short. As much as I was hoping to break you first I will have to settle for just killing you."

Daemon's hand moved from her face to wrap around her throat. He slowly started to squeeze the life out of her, determined to make her death as painful as possible because Zamira knew that he could have easily snapped her neck in a second.

Zamira thrashed with what little movement the restraints would allow, but she didn't have enough leverage to even hope to dislodge his death grip. The world started to fade around the edge of her vision and she wondered if she could watch Akia from the other side of life.

As Zamira began to give in to the encroaching darkness, the great wooden door shattered in a shower of splinters. On the other side she glimpsed the shadow of a great beast silhouetted against the light of the corridor.

Air suddenly rushed back into her lungs as Daemon turned to address this new threat.

"Akia…," she whispered as she lost her battle with consciousness. She could have sworn that she heard a roar before the blackness took over.

CHAPTER TWENTY-FIVE

Akia had been right. Using his name, the native rebels were able to secure some of Batu's troops. Despite some understandable wariness on the part of the rebels, the added manpower allowed them to hit all three targets simultaneously. Rolo was leading Akia, Jax, and two other rebel fighters to the tower in which Zamira was being held hostage. The journey took longer than they would have liked because the tower was in Daemon's personal quarters. While the servants in the rest of the palace just moved out of their way, the servants and soldiers in this wing actually fought them. Power in any form garnered followers and the intelligent leaders kept the most zealous nearby.

None of the people they encountered were a match for Akia in his fury, but sheer numbers slowed them down. They were just a few floors away from the Zamira's prison at the top of the tower when the energy shields fell. Obviously one of the three targets housed the generators. The commander in Akia briefly wondered what was found in the other two targets.

The attacks from the fighters in the sky no longer exploded in the air above the palace. Their blasts shook the ancient stone walls as they found their true targets. Akia and his comrades had to brace themselves against the stairwell wall to keep from tumbling down the steps. Dust rained down on them from above. Akia hoped Batu's fighters became more judicious in their targets now that their blasts hit true, otherwise they would bring down the entire structure.

Akia continued up the stairs; a feeling of urgency filled his heart and mind. The men heard shouting form above and were nearly bowled over as screaming servants ran down the stairs from the rooms above. A second explosion rocked the foundations of the tower sending the fleeing people into a panic.

Akia had plastered himself against the wall to avoid getting caught up in the tide of escapees. They were on the floor below the area Rolo said Zamira was being held when Akia's enhanced hearing heard a feminine cry of pain.

His heart seized. He would know that voice anywhere. Fur rippled across Akia's skin. Zamira was hurt and that was unacceptable. Akia started shoving the fleeing people out of his way, shifting into his phased form as he moved. Even though the others had not heard Zamira's cry above the din of battle and fear, they fell into formation behind Akia, trusting that he readied for battle for a reason.

The rest of the group had a difficult time keeping up with Akia since they had to deal with those individual's Akia tossed aside in his haste. That was how Akia found himself standing alone in front of a thick wooden door. Akia closed his eyes and inhaled. The exotic floral fragrance that was purely Zamira filled his being. The scent was fresh and tinged with fear. He knew without a doubt that Zamira was behind that door.

He tried the handle only to find it locked. Of course it wouldn't be that easy. He laid his head against the door to hear the muffled voices within.

"…I will just have to settle for killing you."

Daemon was in the room with Zamira. Akia knew he was responsible for her cry of pain and now he was going to kill her.

Akia looked the door over. It was ancient and thick, made of some sort of hardwood. To a native it would be difficult to breach. But Akia was Vukasin and his strength had been honed in the hell of the arena. This door was nothing compared to the metals of the cages they had placed him in before.

Akia backed up to the other side of the hallway and pushed off the stone wall to increase his momentum. With the force of rhino-bear he hit the door. Wood exploded into the room as pieces of the door hung from the mangled hinges.

Light from the hallway spilled into the darkened room to illuminate Daemon looming over a trussed Zamira, his hands wrapped around her neck. Daemon jumped away from the woman to face the threat at the door but the damage was done. Zamira let out a hoarse whisper of "Akia..." before collapsing, deathly still.

Akia roared his rage and charged Daemon, intent on tearing the bastard apart with his bare hands. Daemon grabbed a stun stick from his cabinet of torturous toys and jabbed Akia with it. The pain was but an annoyance to Akia, since it was just a single stunner; but Daemon used the weapon to leverage Akia away from him long enough to hit a stone brick on the wall.

That brick triggered a mechanism that opened an

escape route which Daemon wasted no time getting into. Akia followed on Daemon's heels but bounced off of an energy shield and had to watch in frustration as the hidden door slide shut on Daemon's retreating form.

Akia turned to the trigger stone, but it refused to open a second time. It most likely had been programmed for a single use. Akia roared. Daemon would not escape him this time. He would take the palace apart if he had to. That was why the rest of the rescue troop found Akia tearing the wall apart with his bare hands stone by stone.

Rolo rushed over to the prone high priestess and checked her pulse. He sent a prayer to the Goddess Ti'lak when he found her to still be alive.

"She lives," Rolo called to the room.

Jax laid a hand on Akia's shoulder. Akia turned on him snapping his fangs in his face with a snarl. No one had the right to interfere in his revenge.

"Your mate is alive, Akia. You must care for her."

The beast's head turned to the bed where Zamira lay. Rolo was leaning over her trying to unfasten the restraints that held her spread eagle across the bed. Snarling, Akia launched himself across the room and covered Zamira.

One of the natives raised their weapon to fire at Akia. "He's going to kill her."

Rolo backed away from Zamira and placed a hand on the barrel of the rebel's gun. "No, look."

The rebels watched as the fearsome Vukasin Beast gently removed the restraints and gathered up the unconscious priestess. Clawed hands that were made to rend and tear caressed her face softly. The beast held her close with a keening cry. He held her close, rocking back and forth as his claws sweetly brushed though her hair.

"Come back to me, *jinaria mio*," the beast's voice was gruff and distorted as he spoke through the fangs in his mouth. "You must come back. Without you the universe holds no meaning. Without you the beast wins and I will truly become the monster everyone fears." Tears pricked his eyes. He couldn't lose her, not when he had just found her.

Zamira stirred in Akia's furry arms and her eyes fluttered open. She raised one delicate hand and caressed Akia's cheek. Akia closed tear filled eyes and leaned into her touch.

"My beautiful beast, you came for me," she whispered through her damaged throat.

"I will always come for you, my love."

Another explosion caused part of the roof to

collapse, interrupting the couple's tender reunion. Akia covered Zamira with his body, protecting her from the falling debris. He grunted but did not complain when a particularly large stone hit his shoulder before falling onto the bed next to them.

"It is time to leave, High Priestess," Rolo motioned to the door.

Akia stood gathering Zamira into his arms.

"I can walk, you know." Zamira snapped her mouth shut and didn't protest further with the quelling look that Akia gave her. They followed behind Rolo, jogging at a pace that Zamira would have had difficulty keeping up with. Of course she would never admit that to Akia and his high handed ways.

Dust and dislodged stones littered the darkened interior of the palace. The sounds of their breathing and feet hitting the stone floor echoed eerily in a quiet only disturbed by the occasional explosion. The silence had Akia's hackles up. There should have been at least a little bit of resistance. What was Daemon planning?

CHAPTER TWENTY-SIX

Light spilled through the massive gate at the front of the palace. The rescue team blinked as their eyes adjusted to the bright light of the outside. Huge warriors emerged from the shadows of the jungle, surrounding their group.

Zamira shrank into Akia's arms with a whimper, thinking the Vukasins she was seeing were Tanis. Daemon would kill her if she was captured again.

"Be calm, *jinaria*. They are on our side."

Zamira looked up at the man who held her heart. He was still in his phased form, but she found him beautiful. His eyes were the same midnight blue no matter his form. In this form dark grey fur with black tips covered his body. It was surprisingly soft. He once again wore the metal collar around his neck that all of the Vukasin warriors seemed to favor. She could feel the boney plates that covered his spine. Their almost stone like texture was an interesting juxtaposition against his luxurious fur. He was her strength; as long as Akia was with her she could face anything.

Zamira patted his arm and pointed down. Reluctantly Akia lowered her to the ground so she could stand on her own two feet. She stood tall next to Akia, well as tall as someone as tiny as she was could manage, as a man moved towards them. Despite her torn clothes and tiny stature, she gave off a regal air.

The Vukasin soldier bowed to Akia. "*Kijani*."

Akia acknowledged him but motioned for him to wait a moment. Akia kneeled in front of Zamira and laid his head against her, wrapping his arms around her waist.

He whispered so only she could hear, though she had to strain to understand his speech as he spoke through his phased lips, "I thought I had lost you, my

love. From now on I will always be by your side."
He rested his head there a moment before sighed and
looked up into her eyes. "Sing for me, *jinaria*. What
comes now would be easier as a man, but without
your song I struggle to be a man again and I am not
sure I could manage it on my own right now."

Zamira blinked back tears. It took a truly strong
man to be willing to admit when he needed help
from someone else. Akia needed her but he felt that
she needed to know his emotions first. She was
humbled by this giant of a man. He wasn't afraid or
ashamed to claim her in the gentlest ways in front of
his own people. Could she do any less for him?

Her hand reached up to his face and he leaned
into her touch like a man who had been starved of
affection. She placed a kiss on the side of his furry
face, near his fearsome fangs, without fear. Her
song started as a simple hummed tune against his
skin. But she gently raised the volume, until she
added words old and ancient recognized by any
native of Ludus Prime.

The men and women of Ludus Prime, who were
mingled with the warriors from Vukasin, collectively
gasped. Their high priestess was singing the ancient
wedding chant. That chant was rarely sung these
days as few committed themselves for life to
another. She was claiming before the people that
this was the man she had chosen. She chose him
before all others. She was committing a lifetime to
someone they all feared; someone from outside of

their world. They needed the priestess to unite their people, what would this union mean to their world?

As the song progressed, Akia's face changed and his fur receded. By the time the last note hung in the air, a man, not a beast, was kneeling before Zamira. The two gazed at each other as if they existed in their own world instead of being surrounded by a multitude of people. Man and woman alike watching the scene unfold secretly hoped to someday find someone to look at them the way Zamira and Akia look at each other.

The spell was broken as the Vukasin commander cleared his throat, "*Kijani* Akia. We have medics by the transport to see to your wounds. Also, the *Khalon* as well as your brother are insistent on speaking with you."

Akia stood tucking Zamira beneath his arm. He felt her wince as the laceration across her stomach rubbed against his borrowed uniform. He looked down at Zamira and gave a gentle smile. She was his first priority.

"Tell Banji and the *Khalon* that they will have to wait a while. I will take care of my mate first." He and Zamira started walking towards the medic station. He called over his shoulder to the imperial soldiers, "and see if someone can find me a different uniform. I want to rid myself of Daemon's stench."

The soldiers began moving to complete their

various tasks. Some directed the rebels to medics while others helped them gather what equipment they had. A group of soldiers surrounded Jax as he was a Vukasin in a Tanis uniform and they did not recognize him. A few of the soldiers acted hostile, barking orders and raising their weapons.

Jax didn't resist but raised his hands in the air with a resigned sigh. One soldier shoved an energy blade under Jax's nose. Jax looked up only to have the blade disappear as its wielder was snatched away and thrown. An angry Akia glared at the remaining soldiers and Jax noticed the rebels had formed a ring with their own weapons drawn.

"Do. Not." Akia growled as the imperial soldiers swung their weapons towards the rebels surrounding them.

"What is going on here?" The none too happy commander trudged back into the clearing.

"Since when do imperial troops treat their comrades with disrespect?" Akia turned slowly on his heel, every inch the Tiaret officer questioning a subordinate's leadership skills.

"He is a Tanis," the commander stuttered.

"An honorable man is an honorable man no matter the species or clan he was born into. Jax may be a Tanis but he is one of the most honorable men I know; and I will have him treated as such or you will answer to me!"

All of the soldiers cringed at the bite in Akia's voice and hung their heads. Even good men had their prejudices. It would take time to undo the fear and suspicion that the actions of the Tanis elites had caused.

Akia motioned for Jax to follow him. It would probably be best for Akia to keep the young man close until the imperial forces actually got to know him. 'What a *frexing* mess,' Akia thought as he stalked back to the waiting Zamira.

CHAPTER TWENTY-SEVEN

Zamira and Akia were alone in one of the temporary shelters the Vukasins had erected. The medic had healed the cut across her stomach and ran a regen unit across her throat. She was still bruised and sore, but on the whole healthy.

Akia was slowly bathing her with a damp cloth trying to remove all traces of Daemon's scent. He was incredibly gentle for such a large and dangerous man. He had even found clothing for her to change into later to replace her torn dress. Injury and rags…none of that bothered her. The fact that Akia had refused to look her in the eyes since they had shut themselves off in the shelter, now that bothered her.

Zamira stilled his hand by laying hers on top of his. She paused a moment hoping that the motion would have him look up at her from his spot kneeling at her feet. But he kept his eyes downcast.

She sighed, "I know something is bothering you. Please talk to me, Akia."

"My *Khalon* wants me to return to Vukas."

"Khalon? That is like our king, yes?"

Akia turned his hand over, entwining her fingers with his, as he nodded. Zamira's heart seized. She had claimed him in front of her people. Granted it wasn't in the grand temple where lifelong commitments were meant to be made before the goddess, but she hadn't expected him to leave her so soon. To be fair, he probably didn't know the significance in the song she sang but he must have felt the emotion held within it.

Zamia extracted her hand from his and wrapped it around her midsection. He was receiving a command from his ruler; plus, she knew that his family was waiting for him back on his planet. She knew she was being selfish but she couldn't help the way she felt. Tears welled up in her eyes.

Akia finally looked up when her tears fell silently on the floor in front of him. Instantly he was up and wrapped his arms around her. Zamira no longer tried to keep her tears silent and hung on to Akia, sobbing into his chest.

"Shhh, *jinaria.* Why the tears?"

"Because I'm a horrible selfish woman and I don't want you to leave me," Zamira wailed between hiccupping sobs.

Hope bloomed in Akia's chest. He hadn't realized until that moment that he feared Zamira would no longer need him now that she was free.

"I didn't think you would need me anymore," Akia mumbled.

That quiet statement stopped Zamira's tears immediately and she punched Akia's chest.

"Of course I don't *need* you. I have never needed you." A frown formed on Aki's face at those words but Zamira barreled through, "I want you. I was drawn to you when I first saw you in the arena. I felt the goddess connect me to you the night Daemon tossed me into your cell. And…" Zamira took a deep breath and laid her hand on Akia's chest and looked up into his eyes. She stayed like that for what seemed like an eternity. She lifted her other hand to

Akia's cheek, which he instinctively leaned into. "I wanted you enough to sing you the marriage song today."

Akia nuzzled her hand until her last words sunk into his brain. His eyes opened wide in surprise and looked into hers for confirmation. Whatever he saw there must have satisfied him as his surprised look melted into pure male satisfaction.

Akia reached up and cupped Zamira's face in both hands. He pulled her towards him, his eyes burning with desire. Zamira felt her entire body respond to the look in his eyes. She remembered that when he had turned away her advances in the cell that he said that as soon as they would be truly alone without surveillance that he would have her. It looked like he was ready to keep that promise.

Their mouths met and their bodies went up in flames. Akia picked Zamira up without breaking away from the kiss and carried her to the narrow bunk that served as a bed in the military encampment. He laid her down and loomed above her. He broke the kiss to examine her as if she were a precious treasure. He slid his hands over the skin exposed by the rip in her dress. Zamira arched into his touch which caused Akia to growl a low sexy growl.

The beast was riding him hard. It wanted to claim its mate in every way possible. As a concession to his baser self Akia grabbed the torn material and ripped it away from Zamira's body. She gasped at the move and he searched her eyes to check for any fear. He never wanted Zamira to be afraid of him. Everyone else could fear him, he didn't care, but if she feared him it would destroy him. He needn't have worried. Her eyes burned bright with desire and longing, he saw no fear. He scented the air just to be certain and was hit with the perfume of her desire rather than fear. She was beautiful.

Akia captured her lips once again as his hands memorized her delicate body. Her hands tore at the uniform that covered him. He obliged her questing fingers by removing his shirt. Akia shivered as her hands left a trail of fire everywhere they went. He was going to go up in flames and he hadn't even gotten to the best part.

Akia moved down her body, his tongue tracing every dip and curve. Zamira covered her mouth to hide the moan that crawled out of her body. He knew she was trying to keep quiet because the temporary shelter offered little in the way of sound proofing. One day soon he promised to himself that he would hear her scream his name.

Akia was just about to start his feast at her feminine core when a voice called for him loudly outside of the shelter.

"Akia! *Khalon* Ghaleb is waiting on the communicator for you. He says he will wait until you speak with him," Jax called out.

Both of Zamira's hands covered her mouth as her eyes grew twice their size. A delicate blush creeped up her body that had nothing to do with Akia and everything to do Jax standing outside.

"Damn it to the five hells, I swear I am going to kill that whelp," Akia growled menacingly.

Zamira couldn't help it, she giggled. "You know you like Jax."

Akia stood up with a dramatic sigh, "His timing leaves much to be desired."

Zamira sat up and retrieved her torn dress, only to discover it was unsalvageable. She raised an eyebrow at Akia who just grinned unrepentantly before tossing her the tunic they had scrounged for her earlier. It was made for a Vukasin male to use as a shirt but came to below Zamira's knees. It would work as a dress for now.

"He isn't going to tell your king no. Go see what your Ghaleb wants." Zamira pulled the tunic over her head and tore a strip of the old dress to use as a belt. She still had on the shoes she had arrived in.

Akia pulled her close and kissed her once she had finished dressing. "You are coming with me, woman."

The declaration warmed Zamira's heart though the delivery left something to be desired.

The pair quickly exited the shelter before they got lost in themselves again. The shelter they were assigned to was set up near the transport ship that had landed in the clearing and acted as a base of operation for the troops. Zamira was impressed by how efficiently everything was run. The Tanis had lacked the discipline of the Vukasin Imperial troops.

"It's about time, Akia." A gruff voice practically shouted at them as they walked into the command center. The man projected on the screen obviously was used to getting his own way in his own time.

"You are Ghaleb, ruler of Vukas, I presume?" Zamira was used to taking control in political situations. The high priestess was traditionally second in power only to the reigning royals. With the entire royal family wiped out it fell to Zamira to step in and govern until they could decide what to do.

The man on the screen blinked and stared as if he hadn't noticed Zamira entering with Akia.

"And you are?" Ghaleb demanded imperiously.

"I am Zamira, High Priestess of Ti'lak of the Hidden Way. I am also the interim ruler of Ludus Prime since you managed to lose control of one of your clans." Zamira refused to be cowed by the man glaring at her. She crossed her arms and met his direct gaze with one of her own. She added a raised brow for good measure.

"Ooo, I like her," a feminine voice laughed from off screen.

"Hello, Megan. How is Abby?" Akia called to the unseen female. Zamira felt a pang of jealousy at the obvious affection in his voice. An obviously pregnant woman with pale skin and flame colored hair pushed her way into the view screen.

"She's is great. She is excelling in her training. Just yesterday she got under Reijo's guard with the practice poles and left him with a bruise along his ribs. I'm so happy we found you," the woman bubbled happily. Another Vukasin male then appeared on screen to wrap his arm around Megan, who then guided her off screen.

Ghaleb gave a long suffering sigh and then leveled his gaze at Akia.

"I'd like you to be on the next transport home, Akia. Batu is more than capable of handling the offensive there."

"You can't take my husband from me!" Zamira growled like a Vukasin warrior and slammed her hand down on the console for emphasis.

Akia smiled at Ghaleb's shocked expression and wrapped his arms around Zamira, kissing the top of her head.

"You heard her. I go where she goes."

"Of course your mate would be welcomed on Vukas, Akia."

Akia looked down at Zamira and whispered gently, "The choice is yours, *jinaria.* I will be by your side no matter what you choose."

Zamira knew that part of Akia wanted to go back to his home planet and she was afraid that he only gave her the choice to make her happy. Zamira took a minute to really study Akia's face. In it she only found openness and honesty. It made her believe that he really meant what he said when he gave her the choice. Was it fair of her to expect him to stay? Probably not, but she was strong enough to admit that she needed Akia, especially with everything she was about to face. She needed to have that one person that she knew didn't have any other agenda than her wellbeing. If she couldn't turn to Akia she would know that every person in her presence was playing a political game with her. She was a sensitive and empathic individual. Without someone to be able to decompress and share her most deep secrets with she would eventually wither and die. She may have told Akia that she didn't need him and that she wanted him, but in truth it was both.

Zamira looked at the view screen with a scowling Ghaleb, who was impatiently awaiting her reply. "I'm afraid we cannot leave at this time. There is too much to do here, especially with the royal family gone."

"Are you certain they are entirely destroyed?"

"Fairly, though once order has been established we will trace the genealogies just to be certain. Until that time I am the ruling body of this planet. I cannot leave in this time of chaos."

Ghaleb wiped a hand down his face and sighed, "I understand your position. You do realize that because it was members of my planet that attacked yours that we feel we have a responsibility to reestablish order there."

Zamira's eyes held steel as she stepped away from Akia and stood regally before the Vukasin ruler. "While I appreciate the offer of help, know that my people will not accept a second invasion, even under the guise of friendship."

"I have no desire to invade, Priestess. I have enough of a headache trying to govern those already beneath my care. What role does my warrior have in your plans?"

"He is no longer yours, *Khalon*…He is mine."

CHAPTER TWENTY-EIGHT

Ghaleb was about to protest Zamira's statement when an explosion rocked the ship. Power flickered and the view screen went black. Rolo and Jax burst into the room as the sounds of battle erupted outside.

"Priestess, we must flee!" Rolo grabbed Zamira's arm to pull her along despite Akia's growl.

"What has happened?" Akia removed Zamira from Rolo's grasp and directed his question to Jax.

"Daemon's troops have rallied. There also seems to be a battle raging in the atmosphere above."

"Five hells. That is a problem, but it doesn't explain Rolo's behavior. This is war, you expect battle in war." Akia kept one arm around Zamira while unsheathing his energy blade with the other.

"Priestess, we must flee now. I have avians hidden in the jungle, but they will not stay for long."

Zamira looked between Rolo and Akia. She could feel the urgency in Rolo but she only felt safe with Akia near.

Jax spoke up again. "Rolo and I were hidden in the shadows as the troops broke through the camp perimeter. We over heard that their orders were to inflict as much damage as possible, but their primary object was the assassination of Zamira."

Akia now understood Rolo's panic. Zamira was the last hope for restoring Ludus Prime's government as she was the only individual that the majority would rally around.

"Let's go then." Akia moved towards the door.

"I only have two avians. I am not sure they could carry you as well," Rolo protested.

Akia grabbed the native man by his shirt and hauled him up eye level. "Where she goes, I go.

Period." He tossed the man down and started making his way to the thick jungle. He was in battle mode; his eyes took in everything. Survival often depended upon being observant.

They were halfway between the ship and the jungle when Akia realized that Zamira had stopped. She stared out into the chaos of men slaughtering each other around her. The Tanis were overwhelming the Imperial and rebel forces through sheer numbers. The ground troops had been a fairly small unit meant primarily for securing a single city as a staging ground for the reinforcements that were on the way. The Tanis had even brought a few of the deformed phased from the arena. Other than Akia, none of the Imperial troops had faced the deformed phased in battle. Their savagery overwhelmed the troops who tried to battle them like regular men. The carnage was impressive even to a veteran warrior. No wonder a peaceful person like Zamira was frozen in fascination.

Akia ran back to her, planning to scoop her up and get her far away from the conflict. He had almost reached her when she stopped the entire ground battle with a fierce battle cry. When she had everyone's attention her voice exploded with a moving battle song. She told her men and allies that victory was neigh, that none could defeat them. While Akia didn't understand the language, the message echoed though his bones.

The last note hung suspended in the air. Even

nature was silent for a moment in the face of Zamira's talent. The world then exploded into violence once again. The rebels fought with renewed vigor, and even the imperial troops took up Zamira's battle cry. The tide of the battle began to turn in the rebel's favor.

Unfortunately, Zamira's little pep talk…song, whatever…put a beacon right above her head. The enemy knew exactly where she was and were heading straight for her.

Akia took off at a run and scooped Zamira up into his arms, throwing her over his shoulder. He smacked her bottom as he dashed for the jungle.

Zamira yelped, "What was that for?"

"Don't ever make yourself a target again!"

"You know as well as I do that if I hadn't sung our people would still be losing." Zamira crossed her arms as she dangled and bounced over Akia's shoulders.

"How did you manage that anyway?"

"I buried a compulsion for the rebels within the notes of the song. It is a form of hypnosis. It allowed me to turn their terror into righteous anger and I left them with the impression that if they rallied they could win." It was difficult to give the explanation as she bounced on Akia's shoulder.

Akia stopped in the dense foliage of the jungle and placed Zamira on her feet in front of him. He cupped her cheek and tilted her face up towards his. He stared into her eyes for a moment that seemed like an eternity before lowering his face to capture her lips in a tender and needy kiss.

"I will admit it was impressive but I don't care. You are my priority, not them. Do not put a target on your head, especially when I am not right at your side to defend you."

"Akia," she breathlessly whispered, "you can't think like that. There is an entire world here that has to come first."

"You are my world. Only you."

Tears shimmered in Zamira's eyes, "You mean everything to me as well and I wish I had the luxury of just being your world, but I cannot."

Akia laid his forehead against Zamira's. "I know, but this world doesn't matter to me if you are not in it."

"I can't run and hide, Akia. No matter how much I might want to."

"Will you still need me when this is all over?"

Zamira looked up shocked and wrapped her arms around Akia, pulling him close. "I will always need you, Akia…always."

The jungle rustled around them and Akia pushed Zamira behind him.

"Then I will make sure we both survive this conflict," Akia declared as he phased.

The enemy launched their attacks and Akia engaged them with a roar. Six assassins had found them. These were elite fighters. Zamira moved out of the way and hid behind the huge fronds of a jungle fern. From the shadows she watched the deadly dance, for that was what this was.

Unlike the base violence of the gladiator arena, this was a dance of masters. Death stalked with each swipe of the blade. All six engaged Akia in rapid succession, not allowing him a chance to recover from the attack of the one before them. He whirled and cut, like he could see behind him as well as in front. Zamira knew he was strong and deadly but it wasn't until this moment that she truly understood just how skilled a warrior Akia was.

Within the first attack three of his opponents lay dead at his feet. The other three pulled back but remained on guard.

"Our orders are only for the woman, brother. Give her to us and we will let you live," one of the men said.

Akia snorted, "I am not brother to you, Tanis scum. The woman is mine."

"So be it."

All three attacked, from three different directions. Despite Akia's speed, he had to sacrifice a blow to defeat an enemy. Zamira gasped as an energy blade skewered his left arm. The blow had been meant to be fatal, taking out his lung and maybe his heart through the ribs. But Akia blocked the blow with his arm as he severed the artery of one attacker with his other hand.

Two remained but Zamira could see that Akia was tiring. If it came to it she could paralyze them with her voice, however, that would stop Akia as well and she wasn't sure she would be able to move the mountain of a man herself. Still she prepared her voice as a last resort.

The assassins attacked again. Akia's blade was knocked from his hand, but it didn't slow him down. He sank his claws into the attacker that dared to get within his reach. He pulled him close and used his fangs to rip the man's throat out, leaving a single warrior.

Akia tossed aside the dying man and reached for his own blade with his good arm.

"Let's finish this," Akia growled.

The remaining man studied the battered and bloody Akia. He must have still seen death in Akia's eyes because he took to the trees.

"We will meet again warrior and see who falls beneath the other's claws." With his declaration, the man disappeared into the shadows.

When the jungle came to life once again, signaling the battle was over, Akia collapsed to his knees. He was bleeding profusely and needed a regen unit desperately.

Zamira ran to Akia's side. "Come on, Rolo and Jax will be searching for us."

Akia stumbled to his feet. Zamira knew that she had to keep him moving until they were safe enough to treat his wounds.

"Why didn't those Tanis shift into beasts like your other warriors do?" Zamira asked.

Akia knew what Zamira was trying to do, but he obliged her anyway as he painfully made his way deeper into the jungle. "Not all Vukasins are capable of phasing. Most that can become warriors. Those men were part of the Tanis Shadow Sect. It is a group of skilled assassins without the ability to phase. While a phased warrior has heightened senses and is stronger, skill is the true mark of a warrior."

Jax and Rolo burst from the shadows and relieved Zamira of her burden. Between the two men they were able to move much more quickly through the underbrush. Soon they came to a clearing deep in the jungle where a hover bike and two avians waited.

Avians were giant hawk-like birds that were native to Ludus Prime. Many generations ago the natives had harnessed their strength to use as transport through the thick jungle that covered most of the planet. As Jax and Rolo brought Akia closer to the birds they became agitated. Zamira was afraid that they would take flight leaving the group behind.

"They smell blood and sense the predator in me," an exhausted Akia declared.

Zamira noticed that Akia was still in his beast-like form. She knelt next to him and hummed a tune until he slowly and painfully shifted back to a man.

The avians settled though they still seemed a bit skittish.

"You and Rolo take the birds. I will follow on the hover bike with Akia," Jax said as he placed a pressure bandage on Akia's wounds to stem the flow of blood. "Rolo says we will be in a safe location by nightfall." He turned to Akia, "Can you hold out until then for us to treat you?"

"I want Zamira safe. Let's get this done."

Zamira watched as the young man and her husband climbed aboard the Vukasin vehicle. She told Rolo to lead the way and she would take up the rear to make sure that Jax didn't get lost in the thick trees. Rolo wasn't happy about the arrangement, but Zamira quickly squelched any dissent by pulling rank. Rolo respected the priestess too much and was too conditioned to obey her position to argue, at least not much. Nevertheless, he still made his feelings clear.

In a matter of minutes, the group was in the air speeding through the jungle of Ludus Prime. They were headed to the most sacred spot on the entire planet. Everyone knew of its existence but few knew the path to get there. It acted not only as a holy site for the priestesses, but historically it was a safe haven to protect the royal family. Now it would protect the High Priestess in place of the royal family.

CHAPTER TWENTY-NINE

He heard the hidden temple long before he saw it. It sounded as if a million voices filled the jungle. But it wasn't the music of nature. These voices were haunting and ethereal. It somehow warmed Akia's soul and the pain he suffered receded. The sound seemed to surround the group and Akia couldn't pin point the direction it was coming from.

"They are expecting me," Zamira called from the back of her avian mount. "That is the song of welcome."

She urged her mount to fly faster, leaving the men no choice but to follow suit. Suddenly Akia was blinded as the jungle canopy broke open to reveal a mist shrouded valley. At the center of the valley he could barely discern an elaborate temple compound, covered in vining flowers. If he hadn't known it was there, he most likely would have missed it. The effect of the echoing voices that seemed to surround them and the mist covered valley…made this place feel like sacred ground. If Akia had been a religious man he would have believed that the gods trod here.

Zamira's avian dived down into the enveloping mist. Rolo followed easily, however, Jax, being unfamiliar with the area, followed more cautiously. It was a good thing that Jax was so cautious because directly in front of them a stone column appeared out of the thick mist. Jax swerved the hover bike, nearly unseating them both.

In and out they flew through the soaring columns. The mist began to clear the closer to the temple center they got. It cleared completely in the great courtyard that was in front of the largest temple building.

Zamira had landed her avian on the intricate mosaic design of the stone floor of the courtyard. Liveried men and women spilled from the doors of the temple. As the temple doors opened, Akia discovered that the source of the voices was within the temple. The volume was thunderous causing the servants to use hand signals to direct Zamira and her entourage into the temple.

Despite his injuries, Akia maneuvered himself to stand next to the woman he loved. Zamira was in her element, standing regal as any queen even in her borrowed and dirty clothing. Her long hair was braided down her back. But her hand still reached for Akia and her delicate fingers weaved together with his.

They walked through the cool stone of the building. The volume of the voices increased until it rivaled the air organ of the royal palace. Sound was truly a sacred part of Ludus Prime. Zamira and Akia emerged onto a raised balcony that over looked the great hall of the temple. Zamira pulled Akia to stand right beside her when he tried to take a step behind. It was a subtle gesture, but it told all who could see that she considered Akia her equal. Jax and Rolo stayed a respectful distance back.

Akia looked over the balcony. He was surprised to see that what he had thought was thousands of voices were actually only dozens. He counted less than one hundred people below. Each voice seemed to be singing their own part of the tune, and despite the number of harmonies, everything resonated beautifully.

The new arrivals let the beauty of the voices wash over them. It was amazing how sound could heal not only the spirit but also the physical body. The spell didn't break until the last note hung in the air.

Without fanfare the singers quietly left the temple's great room. With the welcome party gone, Zamira became all business.

"Rolo, did you and Jax pack a regen unit?"

"Yes, Priestess." Rolo crossed an arm over his chest and bowed to Zamira.

"Take my husband and treat his injuries." Zamira turned to Akia when his growl started. "I am safe within these walls, my love. There are things I must attend to and I need to know that you are healed." As she spoke she put her hands on either side of his face and pulled him down into a gentle kiss.

"Keep Jax with you." Akia put the tips of his finger against her lips. "I have to know you are safe, *jinaria*. You may know these people, but I do not. I do trust Jax, however."

"What does that mean? I have heard you call me that often, but it doesn't translate in the translator."

"It doesn't translate directly…my beloved, my treasure…is probably the closest translation."

That knowledge made Zamira flush with desire and she smiled.

"I will do as you ask, husband. Now go so Rolo can see to your needs."

*****

Rolo proved to be very adept with the regen unit. Akia looked over the suite that he had been directed too. It was opulent in its luxury. Silks and velvets were draped everywhere. Thick rugs covered polished stone floors. The bathing area had been composed of a grotto pool filled with steaming water. After a year of stone floors without even a blanket, the room made Akia uncomfortable.

"Normally these rooms would be only for the High Priestess or royal family. Outsiders wouldn't have been allowed. However, Priestess Zamira has claimed you as her husband and I have seen with my own eyes how much you care for her. So I felt it best to bring you here," Rolo explained.

"Thanks, I think."

Rolo handed Akia a long intricately woven piece of cloth. Akia took it and stared at it wondering what he was supposed to do with it.

Rolo laughed and held his hand back out, "If you please."

Akia gave the cloth back and Rolo directed him to raise his arms. "I'm afraid we didn't have any more modern dress that would fit you and your uniform is torn and stained." Rolo folded and wrapped the cloth around Akia's waist as he spoke. "Therefore the traditional dress was the best we could do since it is wrapped for the individual each time." Rolo stood back and admired his handy work. "Plus this makes a statement for those who will try to remove you from the Priestess's side."

"Why are you helping me?"

"At first I feared you but now I respect you. Both are good in a leader during times of change."

"Zamira will be your leader, not me."

Akia's bare, scar covered chest emphasized his status as a warrior to be feared. The juxtaposition between the rough man and the fine fabric made Akia look like a conqueror. Rolo tilted his head. They needed to make Akia look like a king if he was to stand beside Zamira.

Rolo pulled a silk cord and a servant scurried into the suite. Rolo spoke in low tones as the terrified woman stared at Akia. Akia reached for his black uniform boots. While he had noticed that most people at the temple walked around barefoot, boots were one habit he refused to break. They allowed him to conceal weapons that no one else would know he carried.

"If everything goes as planned the High Priestess will be named our new queen. That makes you king by default. If you remain with Zamira, you will lead whether you wish to or not," Rolo stated.

The servant returned carrying a case which they handed to Rolo before hurrying out the door. Rolo turned, raising an eyebrow at the black boots beneath the elaborately tied sarong; but he said nothing. He sat the case down next to Akia and opened it. Inside was a number of collars and golden cuffs studded with precious jewels. Rolo reached for the most expensive piece but Akia shook his head and pointed to the plain gold cuff.

Rolo picked up the piece and handed it to Akia. He showed him that it was meant to be worn on the bicep. The cuff was fashioned in such a way to be adjustable. But it was still nearly too small. Rolo made note to have another specially made in the simple style Akia preferred.

Rolo tried to get Akia to wear the collar as well, since any Ludus males would jump at the chance to wear a royal collar. Akia waved him off and eventually Rolo had to give up. Even without the collar, Akia gave the impression of a warrior king. And truthfully, Akia may have been right about not wearing the royal collar. This way it would seem less like the Vukasin were conquering if the power appeared to reside only with Zamira.

"Well you are as ready as you will ever be, I

suppose." Rolo clapped Akia on his back. "Don't look like you are about to face your executioner. Let us go find your lady."

CHAPTER THIRTY

Akia had to call on long buried memories of politics and protocol. It may not be civilized but there was a simplicity to "I'm bigger and strong than you so I make the rules." Thankfully Zamira had the civilization that he had lost.

So Akia just stood behind Zamira's chair after the various factions had voiced their opinion that an alien had no business taking part in matters of government. It had been meant to be a strong arm tactic to demonstrate that Zamira would be nothing more than a puppet ruler if they instated her. These people had sorely miscalculated the quiet strength that Zamira had cultivated during her time as high priestess.

She had simply stood and announced that if they were going to bar her husband from actively supporting her then they would need to find another figurehead. Everyone assembled, including Akia, knew that the populace was conditioned to pledge allegiance to a royal line. With that line completely destroyed they had to find someone who could rally everyone, or at least the majority of the common citizens. Otherwise the planet would fall into civil war as factions tried to raise their own political figurehead. Civil war during an enemy occupation would have been a sure death sentence for Ludus Prime and the remaining politicians knew it. As much as they wanted to ensure their own way of life, they knew they would never keep any amount of power if they became a conquered people.

The only people who had a chance to unite the masses under a new dynasty was the clerics of Ti'lak. The religion permeated most aspects of daily life on Ludus Prime. The priestesses were respected and well-loved for their gentle guidance. As high priestess and the most powerful siren born in known history, Zamira was really the only choice to secede the royal family and fill the hole that their loss had created.

Once Zamira gained control of the meeting, she outlined a solid plan for the reconstruction of Ludus Prime. Interestingly enough, she didn't want to create a theocracy. She wanted to maintain a certain separation between church and state and planned to appoint another to act as high priestess should she be elected to rule. She also pointed out the advantages that having her husband on their side would present.

"We do not need the Vukasins meddling in our affairs," An elder woman said, pounding her fist on the table. "It was the Vukasins who destroyed our royal family in the first place."

"Honorable Elder, it is true that a rogue faction of Vukasins were the cause of our down fall, a situation that their ruler is trying to rectify. I have seen the soldiers battling on our behalf myself in the capital city."

One of the few men assembled sneered at Zamira and then shifted his gaze to Akia behind her chair, "So you expect us to let them loot our world while you spread your legs for them like a whore?"

Akia moved so swiftly that no one noticed until he had his hand around the man's throat and lifted him to dangle in the air.

"You may disparage me and my people all you like for it is not without just cause. Gods know that you have experienced the worst of us. But I will allow no insult to my mate." Zamira stood and laid a hand on Akia's arm. She silently shook her head and motioned for him to put the man down. Akia released his grip dropping the man.

As the man wheezed and coughed while rubbing his throat, Akia leaned down so he was nose to nose with the man. Through clenched teeth Akia growled, "Speak to her with disrespect and I will end you. Are we clear?"

Every head in the council chamber nodded. The huge man frightened them, but they also found it telling that he had not interfered when the elder woman spoke out against the Vukasin alliance; but had swiftly attacked only when Zamira was verbally assaulted. It was obvious that the soon to be queen had a very strong champion in Akia.

"Honorable Elders, just a few years ago we had the luxury of ignorance," Zamira walked to the head of the table while Akia resumed his post at her back. "We thought we were the center of the goddess's creation. Who knows, perhaps it was that arrogance that led to our downfall. Regardless of why, our eyes were opened and we discovered that we are not unique in the universe. But we are infants in this new world. We have not even reached our own moon, let alone traveled the stars. My husband's," Zamira stopped, noting who flinched at that statement before carrying on, "people have explored those stars for generations. Whether we want it or not, we will need allies and teachers to adjust to our new reality. If I am to rule these are things that you need to consider. If I do not rule, these are still things you need to consider for the future prosperity of our people. I would rather meet the rest of the universe as an equal rather than as a slave."

Zamira dismissed the council to consider her words. They would make judgements in the next few days.

When the last elder left, Zamira slumped into the oversized chair at the head of the table and rubbed her temple. Strong hands reached around and massaged her shoulders. She was grateful that Akia was willing to jump in to defend her but she was disappointed at the ugly attacks against her chosen mate. It would be an uphill battle to get the two worlds working together. If the people of Ludus Prime had any hope of being anything other than a commodity to be bought and sold, she knew they needed an alliance with the Vukasin Empire.

"Well that went well, I think."

Zamira's head snapped up at the familiar feminine voice.

"Lali!" Zamira jumped up to embrace the woman who had entered.

"Hello, Zamira."

Zamira turned to Akia and Jax who had entered with Rolo. "Lali, this is my husband, Akia, and his comrade, Jax."

Lali's eyes looked the Vukasin men up and down hungrily. "I can see why you have bound yourself to one of these."

The look and comment made Akia slightly uncomfortable, but Zamira just laughed.

"I really have missed you, my friend."

CHAPTER THIRTY-ONE

It seemed like an eternity before Zamira and Lali parted ways in the great hall. Akia had hung back so the two friends could catch up. And if he was honest with himself, Lali made his skin crawl. She looked at him as if he was dessert and she was starving. To be fair she gave Jax the same kind of perusal, so Akia tried to temper his instant dislike but it was difficult.

Lali left and Akia found himself on one side of the great hall while Zamira was on the other. He was admiring how beautiful she looked in the shimmering silk. The deep purple of her gown played off her pale golden skin and accented her glowing eyes. Golden thread and tiny crystals were embroidered around the hem and created a delicate floral pattern on the short blouse. A golden chain set with precious stones circled her waist and jeweled pins were woven into her hair.

Even wrapped in all of that finery, it was the woman who caught his attention. She radiated peace and compassion; she was the balance to his brutality. She had great power, but never abused it. She was everything good in the universe. Even if they had met under different circumstances, Akia knew that he would have fallen in love with her anyway.

"I love you," a voice whispered in Akia's ear. He whipped around only to find no one. "I don't know why exactly, but the emotion is there filling me up."

Akia turned in a circle and scented the air. No one was here except him and Zamira and the voice sounded like Zamira's but she was on the other side of the room. Where was that voice coming from?

Zamira laughed and Akia could see it but, the voice sounded as if it was right next to him.

"It is a unique property of the acoustics of this space," Zamira explained. "Only the priestesses of the temple know of this little trick. Standing here I could whisper a phase and you would hear it, even if the person standing next to me could not. You can whisper back you know."

"Did you mean what you said?" Akia needed to hear it one more time.

"Yes. I understand if you don't yet...we haven't known each other that long..."

Akia marched across the great room floor and silenced her ramblings with a fierce kiss.

"Woman, I can't even live without you. Don't ever doubt the strength of my feelings for you." He made his declaration between nipping kisses and a roaming hand. "I have a promise to keep. Maybe then you will know that my love for you is real."

"Show me, Akia...show me how much you love me."

Akia's mouth found hers again. It started out beautifully sweet and tender but built like stoking a fire until it burned. Akia shifted position cradling the back of her head gently which was at such odds with his mouth that was insistent and demanding.

His hand tightened in her hair and she gasped. Suddenly he was there filling her mouth, coaxing her tongue to dance with his. Music buzzed in her brain, trying to pull her into a transcendental experience. She had only once gone out of body and that had required hours of meditation. Akia could pull her into the divine with only a kiss. Zamira wrapped her arms around his neck trying to stay anchored in this world. She wanted to experience everything he had to offer.

Akia didn't disappoint as he kissed his way down her throat. He seemed to be trying to memorize every contour with his lips, teeth, and tongue. She never knew that she could feel so much. Her entire body burned almost to the point of pain.

One hand kept her hair prisoner while the other slide down her back to cup her backside. Akia pulled her close and she could feel his impressive erection straining against the folds of his sarong.

"*Jinaria,* I want to love you sweet and gentle like you deserve, but the beast in me is riding me hard tonight demanding the claiming of its mate. I don't want to hurt you," Akia said in a quiet, anguished voice against her hair.

Zamira looked up into Akia's eyes and reached up and caressed his cheek. She held his gaze to make sure he saw the truth in her eyes. "You would never hurt me, Akia. I have faith even if you don't. Besides," she stood on her tip toes and nipped at his chin with her teeth before kissing away at the slight sting, "I kind of like it rough."

Akia let out a groan that echoed and magnified throughout the great hall. A servant popped their head in the door across the great hall to investigate the noise. She beat a hasty retreat when she found her High Priestess's body entwined with her alien husband.

"Perhaps we should retreat to a more private area before we scandalize the entire temple," laughed Zamira.

Akia scooped her up into his arms as she wrapped her legs around his waist. He marched off in double time, punctuating each step with suckling kisses. More than once he nearly barreled over servants. The women all sighed as they passed by.

When Akia walked into their darkened suite, he didn't notice the soft glowing lights someone had thoughtfully placed around the room. He put Zamira down and turned to lock the door. There would be no interruptions this time. This time was for him and Zamira alone.

He turned back towards the room and his breath was stolen. Zamira stood next to the bed, a shimmering jewel in the twilight. She beckoned him with her fingers, a siren's smile on her lips. She knew her power over him.

Akia stalked towards her, scenting her arousal. She wasn't the only one with power here.

Akia reached his large hand towards her, tracing the contours of her flesh over her clothes. Zamira arched into his touch with almost a purr. He slid the veil of material from her head and shoulders, running his fingers through her hair as jeweled pins dropped to the floor. He stepped into her causing her to retreat until she fell onto the bed behind her.

Zamira looked up at him through sultry lashes before closing her eyes and dropping her head back exposing her throat and thrusting her breasts towards him. The submissive pose called to the beast within Akia and he pounced on her.

He caught the front of her blouse, that delicate and costly blouse, and ripped the fragile material in two. Her breasts spilled out and he devoured them, nipping and sucking until Zamira arched off the bed with a primal cry of desire.

Zamira held Akia's head to her breast as her body moved against his. Akia used one hand to unwrap the material that formed her skirt. When he found bare skin his hands kneaded up her thigh until he could feel the damp heat of her most sacred space.

"You have too many clothes on." Zamira reached over him tugging at the knot of his sarong until the material fell away. "Got to love easy access," she purred as she ran her hand over his exposed ass.

Akia disengaged his lips long enough to make Zamira understand. "*Jinaria,* I am about to lose control. I don't want to hurt you. Look into my eyes."

Zamira lifted her lashes and gasped because she was staring into the eyes of a predator. She knew that Akia would never hurt her but she shivered under the intensity of his stare. Without a doubt his world had narrowed until she was the only thing in it.

"I cannot promise gentleness. In fact, I can pretty much guarantee I will be rough, maybe even brutal. The beast is calling me to possess you in every way possible. This is your one chance to walk away."

Zamira leaned up and kissed Akia's chest, laving her tongue across a particularly brutal scar until she reached the juncture of his neck and shoulder. There she bit down hard and Akia moaned in pleasure.

"I want to possess you too."

"No turning back. You are mine!" Akia growled before capturing her lips and plunging his fingers into her hot core. Akia kissed down to the swell of her breast. "I am yours. I am more beast than man but I swear I will do everything in my power to make you happy." He punctuated each declaration with a thrust of his fingers.

Zamira's heart exploded at what he promised. She gave herself completely over to the sensations his touch created. She moaned low in her throat and gasped for air as a tide of feeling began to rise.

"I want to hear you, *jinaria*." Akia followed a bead of sweat over the curve of her breast and down her stomach, pausing to swirl his tongue around her belly button. He would taste every inch of her.

Zamira cried out when he buried his face between her thighs. He used his tongue where his fingers had once had been, teasing her, bringing her to the edge only to back away. He chuckled when Zamira beat the bed in frustration.

"I said I want to hear you. Tell me what you want." Akia's voice rumbled across her sensitive nerves, sending shockwaves throughout her body.

"You know what I want," Zamira growled. She used her legs to pull him back down towards her when he started to move away. "Damn the darkness, I want to come…please…oh!"

Zamira arched her back as Akia's tongue thrust into her with renewed fervor. He added a couple of fingers while his tongue swirled around her sensitive clit. Zamira's hips bucked as a fire built inside her.

Akia twisted his fingers until he hit that particular spongy spot all females seemed to have deep within them.

"Akia!" Zamira screamed in climax.

Before she could come down from orbit, Akia had turned her over and thrust deep into her slick channel. She actually heard him growl as he pumped into her. All she could do was hold onto the coverlet for dear life as a wave of heat built once more inside her.

Zamira tried to raise up on all fours to look over her shoulder; but Akia grabbed her hands and held them prisoner beside her. She was force the lean down with her backside thrust high into the air as he worked her from behind.

Being confined should have annoyed her but the new angle had him hitting her core as his balls slapped her clit with each thrust. Her second climax hit like a tidal wave, washing over her over and over again.

Akia roared as Zamira's body seized around his shaft causing him to lose control. With a final couple of thrusts, he was going over the edge with her. With instincts as old as time, his face partially shifted and he bit hard on Zamira's shoulder.

The beast in him finally started to settle as both of their bodies melted to the bed, residual shockwaves from their intense climax radiating through their bodies.

Zamira closed her eyes. She was still seeing stars flash behind her eyelids. Over her life she had a few sexual experiences, after all part of a priestess's duty was to try and pass along their gifts to the next generation. Sex had seemed perfunctory, a necessity. With Akia, everything was different...it was so much more.

Akia nibbled her neck. "I must not have done my job properly. You are thinking too much; you shouldn't be able to think at all."

Zamira angled her neck to give him better access. "Fishing for compliments, are we?"

Akia's teeth scraped over the pulse in her throat. She had no idea how much her bearing her throat to him turned him on. His soft member came alive again inside her.

Zamira felt his length grow with each beat of his heart. "You can't possibly want me again?"

Akia rolled Zamira over until she was under him face-to-face. He gently brushed away a lock of hair and held her gaze. The predator was still there behind his eyes, but something else was there as well. She could see a longing and vulnerability that took her breath away.

"Make no mistake, *jinaria*, I will always want you even with my dying breath."

Akia's body was magnificent, but it was his words which rang with such truth that had Zamira's body flushing all over again. She moved beneath

Akia, teasing herself on the tip of his hardening member. She hadn't thought it possible to be so wanting so fast. Akia was quickly becoming her body's drug and her the willing addict. She closed her eyes and moaned as her hips moved.

"Look at me, Zamira. I want to see your eyes while I take you."

The growling demand sent more heat to her core. She flooded the way with her longing. She couldn't look away if she wanted to; but she didn't want to. No man had looked at Zamira the way Akia looked at her. She knew without a doubt that she was his world.

Akia slid his cock into her slick heat inch my torturous inch. When Zamira would have helped him along, he grabbed her hips and held her immobile. He was drawing out the moment as if he wanted to savor it for all time. Her channel throbbed and squeezed around him and he had never been so hard in his entire life. The beast was waking and roaring to lose control in their mate.

Other men may not understand it but he liked the fact that Zamira wasn't an innocent, that she knew how to express the passion that blazed within her. He couldn't help feeling smug in the knowledge that even though there had been others before him, he would be the last. He would ensure that he was her best or die trying.

He loved watching her face as he slowly pushed through her nether lips and into the tight sheath. She was so tight that it felt like she was strangling him. If one could die from pleasure he was going to die a happy man.

He could see in Zamira's face that he was stretching her to the point of almost pain, but her eyes glazed with lust and he could hear her whisper, "More." Finally, he felt himself hit the entrance of her womb. He was long and thick, proportioned in size with the rest of him. She was so tiny and tight that he had to fight not to spill his essence into her womb right there. Zamira's eyes closed as she moaned in pleasure.

"Eyes on me," he growled. He needed to see her pleasure in her eyes if he was going to maintain any sort of control.

Zamira's eyes snapped to his. No man had ever been able to command her obedience, except for Akia. She knew his demands stemmed from a place of love and pleasure. If she gave him what he needed, he returned it tenfold. Zamira kept her eyes on him as she willed her muscles to squeeze and release him. Akia threw back his head on a heady groan.

"Eyes on me," she mimicked with a smirk.

Akia laughed, sending his cock pulsing in her. He then attacked her with kisses until she was breathless. Then he started to move, pulling back slowly. He tried to memorize the feel of her tight channel as he slid his cock through it, withdrawing slowly.

Zamira gave a little cry as the head of his cock popped free of her heat. He stared down at her and could have sworn his cock swelled even more at the sight. He could see his bite on her shoulder as well as the little purple circles that dotted the rest of her body where he had suckled and bit. He had marked her good and it gave him male satisfaction to know that the world would know she was his.

Akia trailed his hands down Zamira's arms as her hips moved, begging for him to fill her again. He shackled her wrists and raised her arms above her head, pinning them down with one hand. He used the other to trace down her body, tweaking her nipples, kneading her flesh. He loved how she looked like this...a feast of sexual pleasure just for him. Her breasts jutted upward begging for his attention, arms stretched over her head, hands shackled in place, his marks all over her. She was his...all his.

She started to moan, straining against his grip. Her body writhed, trying to pull him in inch by inch. She whimpered and begged. He was trying to remain in control this time, to give her the tender loving he knew she deserved, but she shattered his control with her needy body.

Akia slammed home in one swift thrust. Zamira let out a small scream of pleasure that shattered his self-control completely. He was rough and brutal. Slamming home, he thrust into her over and over again.

He let go of her wrists to grab her hips and pull her close to him, holding her there as he hammered into her. He didn't let up even when Zamira thought it was too much and she might not survive.

Zamira's hands grabbed onto Akia's shoulders and she held on for dear life. A fiery tsunami was building within her. Akia kept her pinned as he fucked her hard.

Zamira crashed over the edge when he changed the angle of his attack and his thrusts bore down hard over her clit. She was still experiencing shockwaves from that orgasm when another began to build within her.

Through it all, she kept her eyes on him. Thank the gods, because she had cried out so many times, Akia worried he might have hurt her; but he could see the pleasure in her eyes. He wasn't sure he would have been able to stop at this point. She had taken all control from him. This was a mating as old as time, led by instinct. He had found the one the gods had made for him, his other half.

Her breathing was coming in ragged gasps and whimpers. It was the sweetest music he had ever heard. She cried out his name and he could feel her body tensing for another climax. He doubled his speed. He was determined that this time they would go over the edge together.

Akia had his fair share of females from the various pleasure houses. He had even bedded a few wives and daughters during his time as Kavi's spy. But nothing had prepared him for the connection he felt when deep inside Zamira. She wiped out every female from his past. There was only her in his mind. He knew that no matter how long he lived he would remember this night. Her burned into his memory. The way she looked. The way she made him feel. This was his paradise and if he ever lost her, the memory of this night would become his bittersweet hell.

Akia lifted Zamira's hips and her gasp turned into a moan as his cock slid over her clit with each thrust. He thrust deep and hard, hitting that sweet spot deep inside Zamira over and over again.

He watched her as she thrashed and moaned. She was so close. He was so close as well. Two more sharp thrusts and she screamed his name as her body shattered around him. He roared his own release as his face elongated and fangs burst forth.

Zamira watched in fascination as her body convulsed around him. A part of her mind screamed that she should be frightened as those deadly fangs struck but it somehow felt right.

The quick bite of pain as he bit into her shoulder quickly melted into warm pleasure pouring into her body. She didn't think it was possible but another orgasm built below the surface as Akia held her in place. She writhed against his still hard cock, pleasuring herself until she burst one last time.

Akia collapsed on top of her, his face returning to the handsome man she knew. Even as he shifted his weight to the side, he remained locked into her body. He practically purred as he felt the shockwaves convulse around him, like a continuous climax. He watched her as she laid there with a dazed look in her eye. Her body was slick with sweat and flushed. He proudly traced over the marks he left on her. It was primal of him, but the beast reveled in marking his territory.

He wished that this moment could last forever. He would be a happy man spending his hours making sure she was thoroughly loved. He knew that he had been very rough on her. Even if she wasn't an innocent, his woman would still be sore…his woman. He never thought he would have someone of his own. Women were too few on his planet. But now that he had Zamira he would do everything in his power to take care of her.

Reluctantly Akia rolled away. Zamira absently whimpered at the loss of him and reached out for him.

"Shh, I am just taking you to the bath."

"Ugh, too worn out. Can't move."

Akia chuckled as he lifted her off of the bed, cradling her to his chest. "Just relax. Let me care for you, *jinaria*."

He carried her into the large sunken bath. He held her in his lap while he bathed away the sweat and stickiness of their love making. He massaged her arms and shoulders until she moaned in a different kind of pleasure.

Zamira closed her eyes as he cradled her neck to carefully wash her hair. For all of his roughness in the bedroom, he treated her as if she was the most precious thing in the world. Never had she felt more cared for in her entire life.

After Akia had them both thoroughly clean, he lifted Zamira from the warm waters and wrapped her in a drying cloth. He gently dried her hair and body before quickly drying himself. She noticed that she was always the first to be cared for, even if it would have been easier to take care of himself first.

Akia lifted Zamira up and carried her back to the bed. The moon was high and the night was quickly beginning to pass. He laid her on the bed without bothering to redress her. His warm naked body snuggled up behind her, pulling the blankets over them. His arm wrapped around her waist and pulled her close to him.

Zamira felt him kiss the top of her head and nuzzle her hair.

"I love you," he whispered.

Zamira twined her fingers with his and pulled his hand up to kiss his palm.

"I love you too, my beautiful beast."

CHAPTER THIRTY-TWO

Akia stood as sentinel at the huge open doors of the great hall. The council of elders had decided to formally coronate Zamira as ruler of Ludus Prime. Ancient tradition had insisted that Akia take on the role of king but he had politely, if emphatically, refused. He saw relief in many of the various elders' eyes. He would support Zamira, but he had no desire to rule. He knew that Zamira would have a hard enough time raising the planet from the ashes of war.

Because of politics and a hereditary monarchy, Akia still received the title of Prince Consort to the Queen.

Leaving formal rule solely in Zamira's hands had proved a wise decision. As the masses filtered into the great hall, many eyed Akia with fear, a few with open contempt. If Zamira were to win the hearts of her people as ruler and not just a priestess and keep their relationship, Akia would have to remain in the roll of the faithful guard dog.

He let his eyes scan over the crowds. According to Rolo's contacts and the elders, Zamira was the primary choice to take over since the destruction of the entire royal family. This planet was used to being ruled by a matriarchy, so a powerful woman was the natural choice. But with any change in dynasty, there were dissidents. A few believed that familial connections to the previous royal family, not matter how diluted, gave them a right to the throne. If they wanted to remove the primary obstacle to their claim, today's coronation would be the perfect opportunity.

Akia spotted Jax with Lali draped over him and he frowned. He was supposed to be on crowd control duty. He couldn't fault the young man for his infatuation, Lali was beautiful even if she still made Akia uncomfortable. She spent much of her time with Zamira which placed her and Jax together often.

The sound of raised voices could be heard outside the temple. Akia turned to see the Ludus warrior women rush to bar entrance from a group of protesters who were making their way to the great hall. Jax was supposed to be the head of security since Akia didn't know anyone else well enough to trust them with Zamira's safety. However, Akia was reconsidering Jax's position because he had allowed Lali to distract him from his duty.

Akia would have liked to confront the threat himself, but he knew his presence would just fan the flames of the rumor that Zamira would just be a puppet government for the Vukasins. Instead he motioned for Rolo to investigate what was happening outside as the doors closed to begin the ceremony.

The chanting started as two lines of people marched towards the raised dais set up on the far side of the great hall. Behind the line Lali walked in singing in the role usually reserved for the high priestess. Her voice raised above the din and Akia could feel the power in the siren's call. It wasn't as strong as Zamira's but it was still powerful. Jax was enraptured by Lali's voice, completely ignoring his duty as Zamira's guard.

The hackles raised on the back of Akia's neck. His eyes scanned the crowd. He couldn't pinpoint anything wrong, but the feeling persisted. He tried to quietly make his way towards the dais. Few dared to confront the giant of a man as he passed. The ones that did were quelled with a fierce glance.

The song changed. Lali's voice blended in with the chanting and the people filling the great hall took up the chant until their voices reverberated throughout the entire structure. Akia knew the sound carried throughout the valley and into the surrounding jungle. It was an even more impressive display that when Ghaleb had been crowned *Khalon* of the Vukasin Empire. The way the sound carried and echoed throughout the land gave the entire ceremony a divine quality as if the goddess Ti'lak descended from heaven just to place Zamira upon the throne.

Akia had finally made it to the front of the great hall when suddenly at the crescendo of the chant Zamira appeared. She stood at the end of the aisle. She glowed in her plain white gossamer gown. The material fluttered around her with each step she took. The effect made it appear as if she was stepping down from heaven to the mortal plain below.

The closer Zamira moved to the ceremonial royal throne, the quieter the chanting voices became. Eventually, only Lali's voice remained as Zamira ascended the dais and turned to seat herself upon the throne.

Lali sung one discordant note, which had Zamira turning to her old friend even as the head elder placed a jeweled crown upon her head. Lali dabbed tears from her eyes, her voice having broken from emotion. The two women smiled at each other and Zamira turned to face the masses as the newly crowned Holy Queen of Ludus Prime.

Lali's last note hung in the air as the elders disappeared, their duty done. Zamira stood, letting the final sound of the crowning fade into silence. This was to be her first address to the people as queen instead of high priestess. As the second most powerful siren, Lali would take over the duties of high priestess.

"My beloved people, Ludus Prime finds the universe and our world greatly changed from the peaceful ignorance we once cherished. As much as we may wish to go back to those simpler times we cannot. We must move forward, for a people that cannot change and adapt will die."

Zamira stood regally at the front of the stage to address the audience. Even when speaking her voice rang with the gift of the siren. It held the crowd in rapt attention, forcing them to listen to what she had to say, even if they didn't agree. Akia could see where that would be an extremely useful skill for a ruler, but a dangerous one if the ruler had been someone other than Zamira. That was probably why the royal family had remained separated from the priestesses until now.

Zamira continued her impassioned plea for solidarity and patience as their society changed. She continued to lay the foundation of friendly relations with Vukas as they faced the common enemy of the Tanis.

Zamira edged closer to the people as she continued her speech. Akia was impressed at her political charisma. He had observed some of the best politicians from his people and the surrounding star systems. Zamira was in a league of her own. He could tell that those gathered were turning their opinion to hers and would carry that opinion back to spread to others. She could have easily been a cult leader with her gifts.

The most impressive thing about Zamira was that she truly cared for the welfare of her people. Never once had she tried to use her gift for personal gain. The mate bond was still new, but it was growing. Akia was able to catch glimpses of Zamira's mind, though she hadn't yet recognized that she could do the same with him. Even in her own mind the welfare of others came before her own.

"Death to the traitorous whore!" a man cried, as he threw off his cloak and leapt over the people in front of him. He had been almost at the front of the crowd and now he was running up the stairs of the dais a dagger raised high. The trance on the crowd broke and chaos erupted.

Akia tried to keep his eyes on the man as he tried to wade through the sea of humanity to reach Zamira. Where the hell was Jax? The only thing good about the screaming masses was it was hindering the assassin as much as it was Akia.

Akia watched as the frustrated attacker lashed out,

gutting a woman in front of him. He climbed over her body like discarded trash. Those nearest to him pushed away in distress, unintentionally aiding the man by creating a pathway cause by fear.

Two could play the fear card. Akia phased into his beast form and roared a challenge. The entire mob stopped frozen in fear, including the assassin. Akia launched himself over the crowd nearest him and landed at the base of the dais stairs.

"Get the Queen to safety!" he growled at the native guards.

Akia placed himself squarely in the path of the attacker. The crowded great hall prevented the man from being able to deviate from his chosen path as the only clear floor space was directly in front of Akia.

"Out of my way, Beast." The man crouched down into a fighting stance and pulled a second blade from a sheath in his back. Akia could see that the man had training and shifted his own stance accordingly. "I have business with the faux queen."

"Over my dead body," Akia growled.

The assassin smiled a feral smile, "That can be arranged."

He launched himself at Akia, blades whirling through the air. He was fast and put Akia on the defensive. Akia protected his upper body with his forearms since he had relinquished his weapons to help put the crowd at ease. He vowed to never be without a weapon again when Zamira was in public.

The assassin buried a blade in Akia's thigh and then retreated before Akia could grab him. Blood dripped down Akia's fingers as he reached down to pull the blade from his leg.

"From the stories I have heard about you, I had expected more of a challenge," the assassin taunted.

Akia's mind quickly assimilated the information he learned from his opponent. The man was small in comparison to Akia, but surprisingly strong. He was well trained, as his movements were decisive and swift. His speed was his greatest advantage as Akia couldn't hope to match it because of his own bulk.

If this had been an arena match, Akia would have taken his time and worn his opponent down. No one could match Akia's stamina. But this wasn't the arena and he had no way of knowing if this attacker was the only threat to Zamira's safety.

Akia's only weapons were his claws, teeth, and brute strength. All three required his foe to get within arm's reach. Battle strategy firmly in his mind, Akia stalked his prey. He didn't rush towards him, that would have been a waste of energy.

The people pushed themselves back, until they

were a tightly packed wall of humanity creating a living arena.

Akia smiled, this was his domain. He shifted into a fighting stance and beckoned the blade wielding assassin. The man smirked at Akia and did a few showy moves, just like an opponent in the ring. In a burst of speed, the assassin flew at Akia.

By this time Akia had figured out the rhythm of his attacks. So he just stepped to the side as the man flew through the air and snagged him by the neck mid-air in his huge clawed hand. With a single wrenching twist, he snapped the attacker's neck.

Akia turned in a circle, the dead man still in his hand and made eye contact with every person in the great hall until they flinched and turned away.

"Know this…I am the Queen's beast. She has my heart and my loyalty. You do not." He shook the body of the dead man at the crowd. "This is the fate of anyone who attacks my queen. You will find no mercy in me. You will only find tooth, claw, and death."

Akia tossed the body onto the floor. The word "death" still echoed in the quiet hall as he marched out to find his woman.

CHAPTER THIRTY-THREE

"Where in the five hells were you?" Akia said, slamming Jax up against the wall.

Lali moved to intervene but Zamira stopped her with a shake of her head.

"I'm sorry. I shouldn't have left my post," Jax wheezed.

"What were you thinking?" Akia released Jax and

paced away from him. It was a stupid, almost costly mistake, but the whelp was still young and Akia knew he would learn from this. Nevertheless, Akia's anger still burned. Someone had dared to attack Zamira and that was unacceptable.

Jax's gaze flickered over to Lali and he blushed. He didn't say anything. Akia respected him all the more for not trying to shift the blame. Though Akia wondered if Lali was as good a friend to Zamira as she claimed to be given she would willfully leave her friend unprotected to indulge in her own selfish desires.

Zamira's delicate hand landed on his arm. "Enough, Akia. I'm fine and we all are adjusting to new roles here. Let us learn from this and become stronger instead of dividing friends."

Akia sighed and wrapped his arms around Zamira and pulled her close. "I could have lost you."

"But you didn't." Zamira motioned to Jax and Lali that they should leave. "Do you know if he was a lone attacker or if he was part of a faction?"

Akia bowed his head, resting it on top of Zamira's. He sighed deeply, "No, I killed him before we got any information. Rolo is trying to backtrack his whereabouts for the last few days to see if that gives us any clues. It is proving difficult since it seems he only arrived in the hidden valley today. How many people know of this stronghold?"

"The valley isn't a state secret, but usually only the elders of the villages and the clerics regularly travel here."

Akia pushed Zamira away so he could look into her eyes. "If this place isn't a secret then why did Rolo insist that this would be a safe haven for you? I mean the place is called the 'hidden valley' after all."

"It is easier to show you than tell you about it."

*****

Akia found himself descending a dark staircase behind Zamira. It was a narrow fit for the large Vukasin warrior, which told him that this passage was built specifically for the natives. At the bottom of the stairs the pair found themselves in a vast cavern. Akia had to admit that it would be a very defendable position given Ludus Prime's level of technology, but they now had to consider much more advanced threats.

"Zamira…," Akia started to explain that they needed a better plan of fortification than the cavern; but Zamira raised her finger to her lips and beckoned Akia forward. Akia shook his head and followed along. He expected to find some sort of underground fresh water source, allowing for an extended siege.

Instead as they moved deeper into the cavern he

started to notice subtle changes around him. The natural stone walls started to smooth out with tool marks; they were rough at first, then they became highly polished until they shone almost like glass. Dirt floors gave way to stone tile. As they continued down the manmade path, vast works of art appeared carved into the stone. As they traveled deeper that artwork began to change to carvings that looked hauntingly familiar.

Pictograms were so familiar; he could have sworn they were raised directly from the ancient texts kept in the Dyami's sacred library. Why would Vukasin pictograms be on Ludus Prime?

Zamira disappeared while Akia was distracted. When he turned to ask her about the pictograms he couldn't see her. He took off running in the direction they were heading, and called her name. He found the path turned sharply to the right. There seemed to be nothing but a dead end and yet he could hear Zamira calling him from somewhere up ahead.

"Zamira!" he cried.

Her response seemed to come from the other side of the stone barrier in front of him. Akia approached the wall and followed her voice. Off to one side her voice didn't seem quite as muffled. Akia ran his hand across the wall to discover the carvings had been cleverly constructed to appear like a solid wall when in fact they were a doorway.

He moved around the carvings and stopped breathing. Lit from above by a circular opening in the cavern ceiling was a familiar pyramid. After Megan had completed the *Mate Avi Keiger,* Ghaleb had ordered a survey of the facility that at one point his ancestors believed to be the home of the gods. They were still trying to reverse engineer the information storage crystals when Akia and Banji had been sent to rescue Maria. But if he didn't know better he would have thought that this exact structure was also in the carnivorous jungle of his home world. He saw that like the pyramid on his world, this one told several stories depending on the direction in which you read the symbols. All of the stories seemed to converge at one point about halfway up.

Its existence here on Ludus Prime suggested that like Vukasins and Earthlings, the people of Ludus Prime shared a common genetic ancestor. This changed everything. Akia had resigned himself to the real possibility that he and Zamira would not be able to produce offspring. They had even discussed royal inheritance should they not have children.

Only the Tanis had an opportunity to study their genetic compatibility and Bel had to know that the people of Ludus Prime and Vukas were genetic cousins. Akia wouldn't have allowed the scientist of Vukas to study the people of Ludus Prime without their expressed consent, and though Zamira agreed for the sake of knowing whether or not she and Akia could have children, there hadn't been time. The ancestor's pyramid changed everything. Akia knew that is was possible that even now Zamira could be carrying his whelp.

Akia closed his eyes and tried to breath away the beast that threatened to burst forth. Every instinct in him screamed that his mate and family were to be protected above all else.

"Akia?"

He opened his eyes to the worried expression of his mate. He moved to quickly reassure her that everything was fine.

"I'm fine, *jinaria*. The gods just chose this moment to reveal something very important to me."

CHAPTER THIRTY-FOUR

Zamira lifted the lamp high as they traversed the empty metallic halls of the ancient's base. Everything was the familiar smooth metallic substance that the pyramid on Vukas was composed of. The only door that seemed to be working was the one at the entrance halfway up the face of the structure. But it was not the smooth operation Megan described. It seemed that sometime in the past the people of Ludus Prime had rigged some sort of closing mechanism.

"It is said," Zamira spoke reverently, "that many generations ago this place was where the goddess would come down and speak directly to the people. The ancient stories tell of a great war among the leaders, who were mostly male at that time, that angered the divine being. As punishment she caused the land to shake across the world. Volcanoes exploded and the oceans swept away entire cities. But still the people fought one another. Their petty disputes were more important than helping those in need. The goddess even went so far as to curse the people with fewer males to balance the violence they were known for."

Zamira laid her hand on the smooth metal of a nearby wall, her gaze lost in time. "I imagine that this was once a place filled with life. I mean who would not want to look the divine in the eye if they could? I could see a vibrant market leading to the base of the pyramid. Inside would be filled with clerics and acolytes directing pilgrims to where they needed to go. Men, women, and children everywhere.

"Yet, we as a people are weak and probably always will be. With one great quake the goddess left our world and buried the home she kept on this planet. It was only with her departure that the people realized what they had lost and quelled their leaders' ambitions. They placed the royal family at the head of our government and worked for the good of all people. Ti'lak still refused to return in the flesh, but she didn't abandon her children entirely. She created the sirens and gave them the songs needed to lead the people on a path of peace and prosperity."

Akia heard the passion in Zamira's voice. She truly believed that her ability was a divine gift meant for the good of her people. It amazed him how a person with such power had the strength not to be corrupted by it.

He debated if he should inform her of the true nature of this place. Would it change the kind of person she was? Would it change how she would wield her power if she found out it wasn't a gift from the divine?

In the end he decided she deserved to know the truth because it would have great implications for not only her people but his own. He had faith that at her core Zamira would still put the needs of her people ahead of her own ambitions.

"Beloved, there is something you should know…" Akia ran a hand through his hair. How did one crush someone else's faith? "This isn't the home of your goddess. It is an observation station for a race that has long since left the universe. Eons ago those people searched the stars and found themselves alone, so they seeded their genetic material across the universe. We have an identical building on my home world. We found a species on another planet called Earth that also comes from these experiments."

Zamira laughed at him. "Do you think we are so primitive that we have not figured out some of those things? We may not have known who; but we understood this was created by people not a divine being"

Akia ducked his head, "Of course I do not consider you primitive."

"I admit that I am surprised to learn you and I have the same genetic ancestors but the priestesses of Ti'lak aren't just clerics. We are physicians, scientists, historians…we may have the ability to influence people with our voice but you cannot lead without knowledge. Long ago we realized that Ti'lak was just a representation of positive forces within the universe. Just like Mi'dal, her male counterpart, represented the negative forces. In the end it is all about the balance."

"But the story…"

"I told you the story because of it's moral. Ancient stories are lessons to be learned for those intelligent enough to see it for what it is. I am sure even your own race still has clerics that teach through the old stories."

"Surprisingly enough, I found out that our priests also knew that our origins weren't divine. It was a secret handed down for many generations."

"The masses need something greater than themselves to believe in. I would bet that the vast majority of religions throughout the universe started as a way to give shape to the inherent knowledge that one needs balance in their life and their world. Petty wars do nothing but destroy and the balance is lost. If one is wholly selfish the balance around them is destroyed; conversely if one is wholly altruistic the balance is also lost. I want to lead my people into a peaceful coexistence with the rest of the universe. But we have to find our balance to do that. We will defend our right to that peace; but not seek to destroy another's peace. I don't want to raise our children in the shadow of war; however, I will not allow our people to be enslaved by the selfish acts of others."

Akia lifted her into his arms and crushed his mouth to hers, leaving her breathless.

"You are a truly extraordinary woman. You never cease to amaze me with your wisdom and compassion. You are my balance. You are the light to my darkness, the compassion to my violence. I am not whole without you."

"Of course I am," Zamira chuckled. "Who else but an extraordinary woman could tame the Vukasin Beast."

CHAPTER THIRTY-FIVE

Days passed in the hidden valley. Despite the battles that raged in the outside world, Akia and Zamira seemed to exist in a tranquil bubble.

Akia woke before dawn. Zamira shifted against his chest, snuggling closer as if she was afraid he would disappear. His heart nearly broke it was so full of the woman in his arms. He knew he didn't deserve her.

Akia reached up and gently brushed a lock of hair from Zamira's face. She was so beautiful, not just in body but also in spirit. Looks fade, bodies age…but her soul would just grow more brilliant with each passing year. It was already so bright that it burned him; but what a beautiful fire.

He watched her as she slept. If there was a goddess in the universe, Akia had her lying next to him. He ran his fingers through hair as dark as the starless regions of space. Her skin glowed like the morning sun. Her dark brows could express every emotion. He leaned over and placed feather soft kisses on her impossibly long lashes. Zamira appeared almost ethereal in her daintiness, like some magical creature born of legend and myth.

"You're staring," Zamira's voice was muffled against his chest.

"I always stare in the morning."

Zamira's head popped up hitting Akia on the chin. He grunted and readjusted so he could look into her eyes.

"You do? Why?"

Akia tilted his head and looked deep into her jeweled eyes. He could get lost in those mystical orbs. He reached up and tucked her hair out of the way, behind her ear. He cupped her cheek and pulled her down for a searching kiss.

It was little things like no fear of morning breath and kissing her with his whole heart that let Zamira know the depth of his feelings for her. She melted into his touch. This gruff, gentle, wild man...this was home. She would never feel like she was home again without Akia.

"I stare at you every morning because my you are my sun. You are the reason I wake up and go through life every morning. Without you I would wander in eternal night."

"Oh, Akia..." Tears shimmered in Zamira's eyes.

Akia rolled both of them over until Zamira was trapped beneath him. He touched her as if she was a precious miracle. For all of his fierce strength, when he brushed her messy bedhead away from her face, his fingers were incredibly soft and gentle.

They had made love many times since the first night but something about this moment seemed different, more meaningful. It was if they were choosing each other all over again. The marriage song swelled in her heart and she couldn't help the tune humming from her lips as his callused fingers memorized every feature. She closed her eyes and savored the moment.

The pad of his thumb brushed over her lips. He gently pressed on the center of her lips and her womb clenched. She grinned and nipped at his thumb. She wasn't the type to be submissive in the bedroom. Fortunately, Akia seemed to like her equal participation, they had a good give and take between them.

She lifted her lashes and looked into his eyes. Everything in her stilled. He had told her that she was home and in that moment she knew he was the same for her. His intense, piercing eyes...so much like the jungle predators of her home world. He looked at her and she knew that he saw her...the woman. Not the priestess, not the ruler, not a tool to be used or conquered. She was simply Zamira and his eyes told her that was more than enough. For the first time in her life she didn't have to play a role. She could just be herself.

That revelation was amazing and she found herself staring in wonder.

"Are you afraid of me?" Akia asked.

Zamira blinked in confusion. She hadn't been expecting that question. For all of his beastly qualities, Akia was probably the most honorable man she had ever known. She had known that long before she was thrown in his cell. He could shift into battle mode in an instant. He could be deadly if the need was there. But with her he was ferociously protective and unfailingly gentle. She couldn't wait to see him with their children. She hoped for a little boy who had his father's eyes and maybe a little girl...

"…a little boy and a little girl."

Zamira frowned. Had Akia just read her mind?

"Impressions mostly…some images."

"Wha…how?"

Akia's finger tips traced over the faint scarring from his mating bite. He hadn't been sure if using the regen unit would have destroyed the enzymes that allowed for the mating bond but he couldn't stand to see Zamira in pain. He had almost given up hope that a bond would form since it had been days since he had bitten her. But when they had held each other's gaze beautiful images of them as a family with children flooded his mind. He was terrified that those images were his own wishful thinking, until he said them out loud and Zamira had wondered if he had read her mind.

"A long time ago before women became scarce on my planet, the people of Vukas mated for life. During their joining the male would partially phase and bite the female, injecting her with a unique set of enzymes that would establish a mental bond between the two." He touched the bite on her neck. "I bit you and therefore …I pledge my life to you forever."

Zamira waved a finger between the two of them, "You didn't think that you possibly being able to read my mind is something that I should have known about beforehand?"

Akia grabbed her hand and kissed her fingers. "I already knew I wasn't worthy of you. Can you blame a man for wanting to bind his heart and soul to himself in every way possible?"

Zamira still wasn't going to let him off that easy. "Kind of an unfair advantage if you ask me. What if I have thoughts up there that I don't want you to see?"

Akia chuckled, laying her hand over his heart while he nibbled down her neck. "The connection goes both ways and will get stronger over time. And as you learn to control the connection, you can close me off if you feel the need." He suckled over the mating bite, sending heat rushing through Zamira's body.

Are you afraid of me now?

She felt Akia move through her mind. It was new but not frightening. It felt right, like he belonged there.

I will never be afraid of you, Akia.

Zamira felt a rush of emotion...relief, desire, but most of all love. Her own heart swelled as love burst brightly forth. Two souls who had been drifting alone in darkness connected together to bring light to one another.

Zamira grabbed Akia, rolling them both over until

she was looking down at him through her curtain of hair. Akia's lust rose up in her mind, hot and needy. Her own answered Akia's call until they were burning in an endless loop of heat and desire.

She slowly shimmied down his body. Her lips and tongue left a trail of heat down Akia's body. Erotic images flashed through her mind and she wasn't sure if they were hers or Akia's. Not that it mattered because she planned on acting on a few of them regardless.

Akia caught that last thought from Zamira's mind and it sent a streak of fire straight to his groin. He swelled pressing against Zamira's flesh as she moved lower. When his member nestled between her breasts he couldn't stop his body from thrusting up to feel the friction her soft globes gave. It wasn't the wet heat of her sheath, but it still felt like heaven to him.

She slid lower, one hand wrapping around his throbbing member. Her small fist nearly strangled him as he walked the edge between pain and pleasure. He gasped as her tongue traced every vein, lubricating the movement of her hand. When she reached his flared head, he couldn't suppress his moan as her warm, wet mouth engulfed his rock hard cock. God he loved it when she took control.

Zamira giggled when she caught that last thought of his. The vibrations nearly sent Akia over the edge. But he didn't want to come in her mouth, he wanted to bury his seed deep inside her until those beautiful babies from her mind were a reality.

Akia hooked his hands under Zamira's arms and lifted her up his body.

"Aw, I wasn't finished," she pouted playfully.

Akia crushed his lips against hers, his tongue demanding entrance until it seemed like he was trying to meld them into one being.

"My turn," he growled.

He wrapped his massive hands around her tiny waist and lifted her up. He used his strength to position her over his engorged member. Ever so slowly he lowered her down, he wet heat covering him inch by excoriating inch.

Zamira squirmed trying to make Akia go faster. But he was fully in control and intent on torturing her with want and pleasure.

"If you don't get in me now...I swear, I'll..." Zamira's words were stolen from her as Akia slammed home. Her body pulsed and gripped him causing both to cry out at the feeling.

Akia kept a tight grip on Zamira's hips. He dictated the rhythm, slow at first. But it quickly built in speed and intensity. Every time his cock slide through her heated folds, fire exploded though their bodies.

Zamira was riding the tidal wave of sensation. She threw back her head and arched her back begging Akia for more.... faster...harder. Akia watched as Zamira was lost in the bliss of sensation. She hadn't even realized that her hands had started manipulating her breasts as she rode him. It was the sexiest thing Akia had ever seen. He filed that memory away to be pulled out and replayed whenever he needed a little fantasy.

Somehow this woman had become his world in a short space of time. Maybe it was a genetic quirk of his family since the same thing had happened to his brother. He could examine the why and how but it didn't matter any longer.

I love you, Zamira.

Akia watched the play of emotions chase across her face. What settled there was a look of love that he thought only existed in myth.

"Hold on, *jinaria*."

He gripped her hips and began to thrust into her with renewed vigor. He drove deeper and harder until he was filling her up and they didn't know where one ended and the other began. Zamira screamed her orgasm, her body clamping down on his like a velvet vice. The tight heat pulsing around his cock sent him over the edge, exploding deep within Zamira.

Zamira collapsed on top of Akia as he held her trembling body to him. Covered in sweat, their breathing slowly returned to normal as the sun broke through the window.

"What a way to wake up," Zamira laughed softly. She rolled over to lay beside Akia, propping herself up with one arm so she could look down at him. She traced the morning stubble along his chin and watched his closed eyes and face as he began to relax.

Akia cracked one eye open and grinned at her. "I told you that you are my sun, it is only right that you should wake me up in such a fashion."

They both laughed as she gave him an ineffectual shove. Zamira got out of bed to head to the warm bath. She could feel his admiration for her naked backside as she walked away as well as his desire for a second round. It made her smile. It was a great feeling to know she had that effect on him.

I love you too, Akia.

CHAPTER THIRTY-SIX

Akia rolled out of bed to follow Zamia into the bath when an explosion shook their room.

"Akia..." Zamira turned with fear in her eyes. This was supposed to be her safe haven and now it didn't feel safe any longer.

"Dress quickly...traveling clothes, preferably something dark." Akia was already pulling on his uniform pants and boots. Akia activated the Vukasin communicator that they had brought with them to the hidden valley. He had been using it to coordinate the Ludus Prime rebels and the Imperial troops.

"Batu, what in the five hells is going on?" Akia demanded of the wavering holoimage. He watched as the command center of the fleet flagship shuddered.

"I'm a little busy here, Majesty." Akia had insisted Batu call him by his name, but the admiral was a stickler for protocol.

"I get that. We are under fire here too. You said you would keep me informed of any change of troop movements. What happened?"

"I wish I could answer that. Reports coming in have our ground troops pinned down under fire. There shouldn't be this many troops on the planet. It's like they came out of nowhere. Hell, I've got a whole fleet of ships in a design that I have never seen before and our sensors didn't detect a damn thing. It's like they appeared out of thin air. I'd say that the ground troops were using slip steam tech, but without a dedicated gate the amount of energy needed to move that many troops would be ridiculous."

The sudden surge in Tanis troops didn't make sense, especially without alerting the ships stationed in the atmosphere. Akia was strapping weapons on as Zamira walked into the room dressed in pants, a tunic, and a sturdy pair of boots. Akia looked her up and down and nodded.

The holoimage blinked as another blast rocked Batu's ship. "I'll do what I can to hold the space fleet off, but holding the line is going to be a near thing if reinforcements don't get here in time. I'm afraid I can't help you out much on the ground. You are on your own."

"Understood."

Akia turned off the communicator. It wouldn't do either man any good to distract each other. He turned holding out an energy blade for Zamira.

Her eyes widened and she hesitated before taking the weapon, "Akia…I'm not sure…"

"Take it, *jinaria*, for my peace of mind. I will do my best to prevent you from having to use it, but I want you to have a way to defend yourself if you get cornered by the enemy."

"I always have a way to defend myself," Zamira asserted but she took the blade and tucked it into her belt.

"I know you do but I also know that you would never forgive yourself if you used your voice to harm others instead of help others."

Zamira smiled. Akia was always thinking of her

needs even when danger was pounding at their door. Another blast sent dust from the ceiling raining down. The enemy was getting closer, soon they will be in range to be able to destroy the temple. Zamira had to get her people to safety as soon as possible.

"We need to find Rolo and Jax to get an updated report. The people of the temple and visiting elders need to be escorted to safety."

Both Akia and Zamira move down the temple hall at a brisk pace.

"I agree that most need to be moved to safety, Zamira. But the reality is those who are fit to fight, especially any that have any sort of training will need to be conscripted. The royal guard is the only trained fighting force here. You had asked that Vukasin troops not come along until the coronation events were completed."

There was a bit of a bite in Akia's voice because they had argued about that when they were in the hidden valley. Zamira had felt it was important that the people of Ludus Prime had confidence in their ruling class. She was afraid that a large Vukasin military presence would make the public see their government as nothing more than puppets to the Vukasin Empire. Akia had argued that public image didn't matter when it came to issues of her safety.

"I'm not going to argue with you, Akia. We don't have time. I still stand by my decision and consider it the best I could have made at the time. Despite what you may have seen my people aren't as weak as you may think they are."

"I never said they were weak," Akia growled. He whirled around ready to attack when someone coughed behind him. Rolo stood at attention and bowed to the royal couple. "Report!"

"The enemy is quickly advancing from the direction of the capitol city. The Vukasin troops report that a new wave of Tanis troops is coming from the direction of the hidden valley."

"Why the conflicting reports?"

"I don't know, sire...I am only reporting the information that was passed to me."

"What about our people?" Zamira asked.

"I'm having the civilians evacuated to the sunken temple. If no one panics, we should have them all secured within the hour."

"Rolo, arm any civilian capable of fighting. It is going to be quite a while before we might see reinforcements."

Rolo frowned, "But they aren't soldiers..."

"Soldiers or not, one man or woman defending their home can be more fierce than ten hired soldiers.

The fact is we need the numbers. Leave a few as a last line of defense at the sunken temple. Coach them to use the narrow passage to their advantage. The enemy would only be able to come at them a couple at a time. Order them to shoot them before they have a chance to get out of the passage. Have the rest report to the royal guard. Have the Vukasin weapons that I requested from the Imperial troops arrived?"

"One shipment has arrived, but it won't be near enough to arm everyone. I have no idea if any of the civilians have experience handling them."

"Give them to the guard since they have been through training. The projectile weapons of this planet are just as deadly, so give them to the civilians since they would most likely be familiar with them."

Rolo saluted and then ran off to implement his orders.

"Akia…"

"Not now, Zamira. We can discuss your safety measures after this crisis has passed. I need a detailed map of the area between here and the capitol city."

Zamia pointed down a side hall. "There should be one in the library." She hurried in front of Akia to show him the way.

CHAPTER THIRTY-SEVEN

They were greeted at the library door by an elderly woman who was gathering up various books into a cart.

"Elder Spazal you need to evacuate."

"Bah, you think I would leave this knowledge for those barbarians to destroy?"

Akia raised a brow at the bent old woman.

"Not you," she waved her hand as she moved off to get some more books, "the others."

Zamira rolled her eyes and shrugged. She couldn't exactly force the woman to leave.

"Where are the maps, Elder?" Akia gruffly asked.

"Aisle 6, in the middle cabinet. What area do you need?"

"The area between here and the capitol city."

Elder Spazal shuffled passed him and patted his arm. "Very wise, my boy. Knowledge is power."

She rifled through a few drawers and pulled out several rolled maps that had been wrapped in leather. She shuffled to a nearby table and unrolled the largest map.

Akia stood over the table and looked down. While these maps were flat, since they were drawn and printed instead of projected images, he was surprised at the level of detail they contained. He poured over the first map and then unrolled a second one…and a third.

"Five hells, this doesn't make sense."

The shelves rattle with the force of another explosion. Elder Spazal didn't even blink. She caught a falling text and put it back on the shelf. She moved down the aisle and called over her shoulder. "What exactly are you looking for?"

Akia flipped through the various maps. "I'm not sure but I would know it if I saw it." He started to think out loud. "Troops are heading towards us from the capitol, the capitol is being attacked by troops heading from our direction...There has got to be someplace in between...it would need to have access to a large energy source as well as a large open area for the troop movements." He slammed his fist on the table.

"I would appreciate it if you didn't abuse my furniture."

Zamira giggled as Akia rolled his eyes behind Elder Spazal's back.

The elderly woman plopped another map in front of Akia. "This whole area is filled with subterranean caverns. Looking at the surface maps you wouldn't know that." She flipped through a few sheets until she found the one she was looking for. She tapped her finger on a vast cave network that was deep in the jungle, but also at the foot of one of the high mountains that surrounded the hidden valley. "This network here has a huge chamber. It is also filled with geothermal energy since it is part of a volcanic chain. There are a few smaller caves and various sink holes that were popular spots because of hot springs. Would a still active volcano be enough of an energy source for what you are looking for?"

Akia couldn't help himself; he grabbed Elder Spazal and kissed her soundly on the cheek. He rolled up the map and grabbed Zamira and ran out the door.

"But Elder Spazal…?" Zamira asked breathlessly.

"I'll send a couple of people to carry some of her books and get her secured. We need to find Rolo and Jax, and I need to contact Batu."

*****

"Where in the five hells is Jax?" Akia roared. Everyone shook their heads.

"We haven't been able to locate Lali either."

Akia and Zamira had gathered Rolo and a few captains of the royal guard. As promised three people volunteered to get Elder Spazal secured. She evidently was a beloved fixture within the temple and no one wanted to see her hurt. Once that was taken care of, they gathered in the private council chamber.

Akia had contacted Batu who in turn had patched the leader of the Imperial ground force in. The two men's images hovered above the center of the council table.

Akia unfurled the map on the council table. "Batu, can you post a topical scan of the area between here and the capitol city?" They wait for a moment before the projected image split again showing the scan between the two military leaders. "I believe that the Tanis are slipping in here. I'm also fairly certain that they built a slip stream station in the caverns beneath this mountain."

"A slip stream station would explain the sudden influx of troops; but why here?" the Imperial *Kijani* questioned.

Akia responded, "This mountain is an active volcano and ripe with geothermal energy. A slip stream needs massive amounts of energy and our crystal energy isn't readily available on this planet. Geothermal energy on this scale would provide what they need to recharge those crystals with some fairly simple adaptations."

"That doesn't solve the sudden appearance of an entire space fleet," Batu said.

Akia rubbed his hand through his hair, "Physics of space travel is your area of expertise. I'm a foot soldier on terra firma."

The holoimages filled with static. When they came back on it was to Batu barking orders.

He turned to the meeting and said, "Ladies and gentlemen, could we hurry this along. I'm not going to be able to help you on the ground. I've got my hands full up here."

"We just need to coordinate a pincer move between us and the Imperial forces in the city. I'm planning on taking a smaller group into the caverns to shut down the slip stream." Akia looked over to the ground force commander.

"I'm providing the distraction; I take it?" the *kijani* asked.

Akia inclined his head in acknowledgement, "If all goes well, we can just pick off the ones that are already here with guerilla warfare until we break them."

CHAPTER THIRTY-EIGHT

"I don't like this," Rolo whispered.

"What's wrong?" Zamira asked as they crouched in the shadow of the trees near the cavern entrance.

Akia had tried to convince Zamira to remain safe in the shelter of the ancient alien pyramid. As usual she refused. It didn't matter that she would be safer to her. She felt that she couldn't ask others to risk their lives if she wasn't willing to do the same. That strength of spirit and conviction was one of the things Akia loved most about her. It was also one of the things that drove him mad.

"There should be more sentries. I have only counted half a dozen."

"Which probably means they are waiting for us." Akia tuned to Rolo, "Are all the passages mapped for this cavern?"

Rolo thought for a minute and shrugged, "As well as they could be. It is possible that a lava flow could have carved something new that isn't on the map."

Akia considered scrapping the mission. He agreed with Rolo; something just didn't feel right.

Do you hear that, Akia? Zamira addressed only him through their link. He loved that they had that connection.

Akia closed his eyes and concentrated on his animal like hearing.

It's faint but it sounds like someone is singing.

There is power behind that voice. It's Lali! I'm sure of it. How did Daemon's people sneak into the temple without us knowing?

Akia had his suspicions but he didn't want to voice them to Zamira yet.

"Rolo, have the men plug their ears."

Rolo's eyes widened but he didn't ask why. He passed the command along to the others in their party.

"Akia…"

"Zamira, if Daemon is using Lali's power to mesmerize we have to take every precaution; even if she is doing it under duress."

Zamira frowned at his choice of words but said nothing else.

Explosions were heard in the distance. The Imperial forces had engaged the Tanis. That was Akia's cue to head into the cavern complex. Zamira squeezed his hand and fell in behind him like they had agreed.

Akia signaled Rolo who sent a couple of his men to dispatch the sentries. Akia watched as the smaller Ludusites melted into the shadows of the jungle. They moved through the foliage with practiced ease. Even with his keen animal eye sight Akia was having difficulty distinguishing them from the surrounding jungle. It would be practically impossible for the sentries to spot them. The men used the poisoned blow darts to silently take down the Tanis soldiers.

The Tanis soldiers slapped their neck, thinking a

pesky bug had bitten them. Before they could lower their hands back down, their bodies fell forward. Their bodies laid on the ground, one of them giving a few final twitches before becoming still. The group waited a moment to make sure that the poison had fully taken affect.

Akia motioned his soldiers forward. He felt Zamira shudder at his back at the staring sightless eyes of the dead Tanis. Akia had to bite back a curse. He should have insisted that Zamira stay behind, but the truth of the matter was he needed her within his sight after Daemon nearly killed her. So when she argued that she needed to accompany them, he hadn't put up much of a fight. Zamira wasn't meant for a world of death and destruction like Akia was. She was light and love instead. To her credit that shudder was the only outward sign of this being difficult for her. His woman had a core of steel when she needed it.

The group quietly stalked into the darkened cavern, weapons drawn. It was eerily quiet as they went further into the darkness. Akia removed the cloth he had used to stuff his ears from one ear. His instincts were screaming at him that death waited around the next corner. He needed all of his senses to keep his people safe.

He could hear booted feet and voices in the distance. He could no longer hear Lali singing. He motioned to everyone that it was safe to remove the cloth from their ears for now.

As they moved further into the cavern, the natural rock formations gave way to constructed walls and floors. Illumination crystals were placed along the walls to light the passages. It was clear that the Tanis had constructed an entire complex within the mountain. Judging by the lack of natives, no one had known it was even here.

Akia held up his hand at the juncture of two passages; to the left he could hear people walking towards them. His keen hearing could distinguish two separate people, but he couldn't hear any others. Their conversation pegged them as scientists, not soldiers. Why would scientists be here? This was simply a credit making venture wasn't it?

To investigate, Akia and his people needed to get down that hall. He motioned to the man and woman who had the blow darts. The pair stepped into the corridor and let their darts fly. Two thuds were all that was heard. The two assassins dragged the bodies into a side room and quietly closed the door. They held up the crystal devices the Tanis preferred for locking doors and shackles.

With a nod, Akia acknowledged their good work. He took one of the devices as they passed to take point moving forward. As Akia was the only one who could read Vukasin, he directed them to the area labeled as the lab.

A quick survey of the area showed only three other Tanis personnel in the room. The walls as well as the numerous shelves in the huge warehouse-like space were filled with what appeared to be med stasis units. But these units were much too large to house single organs or regenerated tissue.

Akia motioned for his people to take out the lab personnel. He mimed to keep at least one alive to answer their questions. They performed their task swiftly. Before the last man standing realized what was happening his comrades had already breathed their last. While the scientist was physically larger than Rolo and his fighter's he was severely outnumbered and out armed.

Akia walked towards the restrained worker when he heard a sharp intake of breath from Zamira. Akia turned, hand on his energy blade ready for battle. No one was attacking Zamira. She was standing there staring at the med stasis module with her hand over her mouth and a horrified expression in her eyes.

Akia walked over to her and wrapped his arm around her shoulder. He then looked up to see what had distressed her so much. At first he saw nothing through the small window of the unit, so he took a step closer. He suddenly felt sick to his stomach.

You saw him too, didn't you? Zamira used their mental connection, afraid that if she used her voice she would start screaming and would never stop. How could anyone do something so horrible?

"I did." After his initial shock, Akia examined the

stasis unit closely. Floating inside was the body of a male child, a Vukasin child if he had to guess. According to the monitoring equipment, the child suspended in the stasis fluid was still alive, at least in body. The brain was registering very little activity. Akia walked down the row of units and saw that every unit held the body of a male of varying ages from infant to nearly adult. He moved over a row and found much of the same, except some of these housed other species in various stages of development.

Instead of speculating Akia marched over to the prisoner and demanded, "What in the five hells is going on in here?"

Rolo removed the lab assistant's gag and prodded him with the blade of his knife.

Between the point of the blade in his back and the Vukasin Beast looming over him, the Tanis prisoner started to tremble violently. It took another none to gentle poke with the knife before he started stammering, "Th...This is th...the battlefield supply research and development facility."

"Are you telling me the Tanis are using clones as soldiers?" Akia's voice was quiet but held a menacing bite that made the researcher flinch.

"N...not exactly. Each specimen is genetically unique. We found that the genetic material broke down too quickly causing unwanted mutations when direct cloning was involved. We were able to solve most of those issues by mixing the DNA of individuals to create an entirely new and unique specimen."

The researcher's voice became animated when he talked about the process. The science behind it obviously excited him, but he seemed to have no idea of the moral repercussions and did not look at the beings in the tanks as individuals. "We keep their brainwaves suppressed during the accelerated growth process so it only provides bodily functions and basic motor skills, that way when they are activated they are an entirely blank slate that can walk and learn immediately."

"I get why the Tanis would create soldiers, but I saw at least three other species including the Kassis in those tanks," Akia growled at the overly excited man.

"Those were commissions. I don't know the particulars but rumor has it that certain individuals within those species were willing to pay obscene amounts of credits for a home grown army."

"Have you no shame?" Zamira couldn't stand the researcher talking about the people in the tanks as if they were nothing but a product. "Those are living, breathing people in there." She gestured towards the tanks.

The researcher snorted, "Lady, those are only

receptacles, empty shells with no personality, until they are programmed. Then they become the people you want them to be."

Akia had to restrain Zamira as she attempted to slap that stupid smirk off the researcher's face. He could feel her anger burning through their link and he understood it, but they needed a little bit more information.

"How do you program them?" Akia held Zamira close until she calmed down.

"That's not my department so I don't know the particulars. My understanding is they use something similar to hypnosis to lay the foundation then they are sent off to the training facilities."

That is why they needed Lali. She may not be able to reach entire armies, but she has the power to hypnotize a whole room for short periods of time. That is why they took her.

*My love, this has obviously been going on for quite some time...*Akia didn't finish the thought because he didn't have to. Zamira was an intelligent woman. She may want to see the best in those she cares about, but he could tell by the look in her eye that she was having her own doubts about her friend Lali.

The researcher's eyes darted around the people who surrounded him. They had fallen silent and it made him nervous. He just had to get away so he could raise the alarm. The Beast was his main worry, but he seemed to be occupied comforting the woman he held in his arms. The others were merely natives. Even as a scientist his size and strength outmatched theirs just because he was Vukasin.

He had to make a break for it while the Beast was distracted. He sprang up even though his hands were still tied behind his back. He aimed for one of the native women. His reasoning was she was more delicate and easier to overpower. He used his bulk to knock her down and barrel through the opening that created. He barely registered the slight sting where she grabbed his leg. He needed to make it to the far wall where an emergency alarm switch was located. Otherwise the alarms wouldn't sound unless one of the units was damaged.

Rolo was about to take off after the fleeing man, but Akia grabbed his arm and shook his head.

Three…four steps and the man stumbled…five…six steps and he fell to his knees. He tried to move along the ground like an inchworm until he collapsed wheezing from exertion. The wheeze quickly turned into a death rattle, until silence.

"Stack him with the others out of sight." Akia helped the fallen woman up. "Good job. You didn't even hesitate. When we get back, talk to me about joining the queen's security detail."

"What should we do with them?" Rolo waved his hand in the direction of the med stasis units.

"Leave them for now. We will figure out a way to deal with them after we deal with the Tanis problem."

Zamira looked down the lines of men and children as they passed through the facility. *We have to figure out a way to help them, Akia.*

And we will, jinaria. *One thing at a time.*

How could anyone experiment on their own people?

All societies have those individuals that deem the lives of others as less than their own. It is easy to turn people into things when you don't value life.

So much knowledge wasted on war...Imagine what they could have accomplished for their people if their talents were turned to altruistic pursuits.

War pays better, my love.

CHAPTER THIRTY-NINE

Zamira followed Akia as they moved out of the lab and down a darkened corridor. On either side the way was lined with numerous cells reminiscent of the gladiator slave cells. Zamira didn't dare peak in for fear of finding something she couldn't ignore and endangering their mission. While the lab had answered some questions about where the Tanis were getting the influx of manpower, she agreed with Akia that there was still most likely a slip stream depot because so far they hadn't found a place for equipment production. This meant that the weapons and supplies were being sent to Ludus Prime some way.

Time was running out, but the mountain complex was much more extensive than any of them had anticipated.

The group came upon a junction which led to numerous halls.

"Where do we go now?" Rolo asked. "And why are there not more personnel for such a large operation?"

Akia shook his head and looked around warily. "I don't know." He suddenly grabbed the communicator out of the pocket of his pack. "Akia, here."

"*Kijani,*" a voice crackled across the communicator. It was difficult to hear since Akia had the volume turned down to prevent it from giving away their location should the enemy pass by. "We are taking heavy casualties. I've never seen Tanis like this before, they seem to have a death wish. They are using suicide bombers to take out as many of my men as possible. At this rate, we have maybe half an hour before I will have to retreat."

"Understood. Do what you can and we will see what we can do from here." Akia shut off the communicator. "Change in plans. The slip stream has become a secondary target rather than a primary target. We need to figure out where and how they are programming these test tube soldiers and put a stop to the numbers. And fast"

"We would cover more ground if we split up," Rolo said.

"Do we have enough explosives to have everyone pair off and each team have a bomb?" Akia asked.

"It would only be one per team, but yes."

"Do it. If you happen upon the slip steam depot, take it out. If you find where they are programming these soldiers activate your communicators and the rest of the team will converge there. Understood?" Akia looked over the men and women who had come on this mission. Each nodded before pairing off and heading down one of the halls.

Akia and Zamira were left alone with three remaining unexplored halls. They were trying to decide which hall to choose when Akia suddenly lifted his head.

He pointed to the middle hall, "That way. I hear singing down that hall."

Zamira strained to hear what his heightened senses heard. It was barely audible but she could hear the faint strains of a melody. Akia took the cloth he had used in his ears at the cave entrance and stuffed them into his ears once more.

Communicate with me through our link so I can hear you, Akia said.

You think that Lali is the one programming the manufactured soldiers. Zamira and Akia started moving carefully down the hall. They had no way of knowing how far they had to get to find the source of the voice.

I do…I know she is your friend…

It's alright. The evidence is mounting that she is a part of this. I just don't know if it is willingly or not.

Akia did not state his opinion on this matter and Zamira was grateful. She knew that she would be confronting some uncomfortable truths soon, but for now she wanted to keep her illusion of childhood friendship.

If I am there we might be able to save those poor men. They were never given a choice. I could give that to them. Zamira's voice in Akia's head was quiet. He could feel her need to find something positive in what they were about to face.

I make no promises, but we will try.

They crept down the eerily deserted hall. Tiled floors gave way to natural stone. Stalactites hung from the ceiling. The end of the corridor opened into a vast and glittering chamber. At one point this had probably been a magma chamber for the volcano whose mountain this facility was housed in. The walls were melted volcanic glass.

The glass reflected not only light but sound as well. The natural acoustics of the chamber were nearly perfect; making it the ideal staging ground for mass hypnosis using sound. A raised stage was at the far end of the chamber.

There's Lali. Zamira pointed to the far end of the cavern where her childhood friend stood wearing a garish, if expensive, outfit. Her hands were raised and she was chanting. The modulations holding a compulsion to adore her as well to incite violence.

Look. Akia pointed behind Lali. There was the young Jax, standing with a vacant expression on his face. The poor boy had been twisted by Lali's power. Akia berated himself for not seeing it sooner. Jax had always acted with honor. He never would have abandoned his duty unless he felt a moral obligation to do so. Lali had used her power to influence him at the coronation ceremony.

Certain events clicked into place for Akia. *Can you hypnotize with a single note?*

No, but a single note could be a trigger for a

compulsion buried earlier. I once used it for a woman who had panic attacks. I buried the compulsion so that when she heard a certain tone she would feel safe and calm. After the session she was instructed to strike a small bell if she felt an attack coming on. That was the tone I conditioned her to. What have you figured out? Zamira felt Akia's hesitancy to tell her what he had figured out. *Just tell me. I'm strong enough to handle it.*

Zamira felt him sigh in her mind. *I know you are strong enough, but betrayal always leaves a scar. I think Lali tried to assassinate you. Just before you were attacked at the coronation she sung a discordant note. She is too much of a professional to do something like that. Add that together with her causing Jax's absence just when he was needed most and it is pretty damning.*

But you didn't find a connection between the dead man and anyone at the temple.

I didn't find a connection to anyone at all, jinaria. It was as if he hadn't existed before that day. If he came from this facility, then that would make sense.

She was my friend...

"I see that her royal highness has lowered herself to see me," Lali sneered in a loud voice from the other side of the chamber.

With the element of surprise lost, Akia stepped out into the open with Zamira.

"Oh look, she brought her pet beast with her." Gone was the bubbly friend and in its place was harsh beauty.

"Why are you doing this, Lali? Why are you helping the Tanis?"

Lali walked down the steps of the stage. Jax trailed silently behind her. All of the manufactured soldiers turned and followed her progress with hollow eyes.

"Why? Why not? We have power, but were never allowed to use it. We were supposed to be gifts to the people. Well what about my gifts? Was I just supposed to give and give and get nothing in return?" Lali laughed. "For years I had used my gift to subtly get what I wanted. I would have been high priestess…eventually, even queen. Yes, even as a child I had ambition. Street girl to queen. It would have been a glorious story. But then they brought you and everyone forgot about me. I was just another priestess in your shadow."

"Lali…" Akia could feel Zamira's distress. She felt guilty as if this was somehow all her fault.

You are not responsible for the choices of others, my love.

"You can stop this, Lali. Our songs are meant for the goddess's purpose," Zamira pleaded. She didn't want to destroy her friend but she would to save her world.

Lali stopped right in front of Zamira. "Why would I stop? You were always the good little devotee weren't you, Zamira. But look where that got you. If you had gotten off your moral high horse long enough to see the possibilities…We could have ruled the world."

Lali pushed Zamira, her face contorted in rage. Akia growled when she put her hands on his mate, only to have Jax block his path to Lali. "You would rather have your beast than power. But I want power. But even now the world wants you. Maybe with you gone, it will want me instead."

Lali lunged for Zamira, but got tangled up in her ridiculous gown. Zamira kicked the woman who she had thought of as a friend and sister away. Akia tried to get to his mate but was met with a powerful blow from Jax.

"Jax…listen to me, this isn't you." Akia could tell from his glazed expression that Jax was under a compulsion. He didn't want to have to kill the young man. His words didn't seem to register as Jax reared back to deliver another blow. Akia hit him hard, sending him flying. Jax didn't even register the pain. He just stood up and unsheathed an energy blade.

With no choice Akia pulled his own energy blade. Each time Akia tried to get to the two women grappling on the floor, Jax blocked his way. The only sounds that filled the cavern were the grunts of the four people battling it out. The multitude of manufactured soldiers stood around them like mindless zombies awaiting their programming.

Lali staggered away from Zamira with a split lip and bruised body. Her fancy gown was ripped in several places and she was covered in dirt from the cavern floor. She wiped the blood from her face and sang out a note. Every male in the room, except for Akia who still had his ears plugged, turned towards her.

Her song was muffled to his ears but he could feel the rising frenzy in those around him. Then he felt, more than heard, Zamira's pure tone. The males near her shook their heads and their eyes cleared as they looked around in confusion.

Lali raised her voice and pushed more power into her tone. Akia looked on fascinated as the males surrounding the women went back and forth between confusion and battle ready. The only one that Zamira couldn't seem to influence was poor Jax. Akia didn't know if it was his proximity to Lali or the fact that he had been conditioned for weeks instead of hours; but Jax was firmly acting as Lali's shield.

Zamira stalked towards her former friend. Her

voice increased in power until it overwhelmed Lali's. With each step she took, Lali backed up a step until they were both on the raised stage with just Jax between them. Akia started towards the stage, resigned that he would have to subdue Jax so they could get to Lali.

He was halfway to the stage when all of the males around him snapped to attention and he realized that he could no longer feel Zamira's song. He looked to the stage to see his worst nightmare. Daemon was behind Zamira with a hand wrapped around her throat. There must have been a secondary entrance to the cavern. Akia ripped the cloth out of his ears so he could clearly hear what Daemon was saying to Zamira.

"So we meet again, little song bird." His hand squeezed Zamira's throat to prevent her from singing. "Fate seems to be in my favor. I have so wanted to continue what we started in the tower."

Akia walked toward them but was hindered by the hundreds of soldiers around him. Lali and Daemon were back in control of the masses without Zamira's voice to counteract their commands. Akia was bigger and stronger than any one of the soldiers, even Jax, but their numbers kept him from moving forward.

"Perhaps we should take this to a more private place," Daemon started to back away heading towards the secondary entrance of the cavern behind the stage. Akia watched helplessly as the love of his life was dragged away by her throat. His keen eyes saw her hand move. She was going for the energy blade he had her tuck into her belt earlier. *Good girl,* Akia thought.

Daemon was too distracted with taunting Akia to notice that Zamira had activated her energy blade. She plunged it into the arm that had her by the throat. Daemon cried out in pain; his grip loosened enough that Zamira could duck her head and get away from him. She coughed, trying to clear her bruised throat, and set out to free Akia.

Lali saw the exchange and ordered a few of the soldiers to grab Zamira. She personally stuffed a gag into Zamira's mouth with an evil smirk. Daemon removed the blade from his arm and stalked over to Zamira, slapping her hard enough to knock her head back and make her knees buckle.

Akia roared with rage. He was no longer trying to save any of the hypnotized soldiers. His only thought was to get to Zamira. He started breaking bones, snapping necks, and throwing men out of his way. The vast numbers made his progress painfully slow. He watched Daemon pick up Zamira and sling her over his shoulder. It was the arena all over again.

Akia watched Zamira disappear with Daemon as soldier after soldier piled on top of him. When she disappeared from his sight, something broke in his mind and he phased into the beast. He exploded from under the massive dogpile of soldiers, sending them flying through the air.

Tooth and claw found flesh and ripped a bloody path to the stage. Akia still moved forward even after a horrified Lali sung the order to shift and all of the soldiers phased into battle beasts.

Lali didn't know about Vukasin anatomy. She didn't know there was a reason most soldiers wore the battle collars around their necks. None of these imitation soldiers had a battle collar. When she called their phased state forward she unknowingly gave the advantage to Akia because when a Vukasin phased, it pushed a bundle of nerves near the surface. When hit, those nerves short circuited the man's nervous system temporarily paralyzing him. Akia had been trained since childhood how to hit those nerves when exposed. It was a simple matter for him to make his way through the mindless throngs of the phased soldiers.

Akia set one foot on the stage only to be hit with a pulse shield. It knocked him back, but he was on his feet quickly to face the threat. In front of him was Jax with a pulse shield on one arm and an energy blade in his opposite hand, flared to sword length. He looked every inch the warrior protecting the maiden as Lali directed him from behind.

"Don't make me do this, Jax," Akia pleaded as he stood up into a fighting stance. He thought he saw Jax's eyes clear for just a moment, before he crouched down and readied himself for Akia's attack.

"I don't have a choice, Akia."

"There are always choices, Jax. You know that."

Jax hesitated but Lali screeched a note behind them and Jax's eyes glazed over once again. She ordered him to kill Akia. Without the hesitation from before, Jax launched his attack. The boy was smaller than Akia, but he was skilled. He had Akia on the defensive early on.

Akia was wasting time trying to find a way to save the young man that he had called friend. Jax was serious about killing him and Akia had to get serious too. He maneuvered Jax into a corner where the bulk of his shield became a liability; forcing Jax to throw away his shield. Without its protection Akia went on the offensive. He didn't even register the cutting blows of the energy blade as he stalked close to Jax.

He pinned Jax to the wall with his body. He gripped his sword hand and deactivated the blade pinning it between them. He tried one last time to break through Lali's spell on him. But he couldn't get through. Those glazed eyes looking back at him were not the kind, laughing eyes of the man he knew. When he felt Jax's hand shift to reactivate the blade, he had to resign himself to the boy's death.

Akia put pressure on Jax's hand shifting the angle of the blade just enough that when he activated it the blade plunged into Jax's chest and not Akia's.

Blood bubbled up in Jax's mouth from the pierced lung and his eyes finally cleared. Tears swam in the dying boy's eyes as he tried to gasp out an apology. Akia calmed him telling him that he forgave him. He held Jax until he breathed his last breath. With tears falling from his eyes, Akia closed the dead eyes of his young friend. This would end today.

He gently laid Jax's body down then stood to face Lali. Lali frantically backed away seeing death in Akia's eyes. She tried to entrap him with her voice. He didn't know if it was her own fear that interfered with her power or if he was immune because of his connection to Zamira. It may have been that the tricks weren't as effective because he knew she was using them. He didn't care. He stalked towards her like the predator he was.

Lali scrambled to get away; her fight or flight response kicked in telling her to flee. She tripped on the remnants of her torn gown and fell off the stage. Akia looked down at her body to see her neck twisted at an odd angle as she stared unseeing at the roof of the cavern. It was better that she had died this way. Now he could honestly tell Zamira that he did not kill her former friend; but she was out of their lives forever.

Now to finish off Daemon.

CHAPTER FORTY

Zamira came to hanging by her arms from a tree branch, her toes barely able to touch the ground. In the distance she could hear the sounds of battle. They must be on the capitol side of the caverns. She twisted in her bindings trying to find Daemon. He was near, she could feel it.

He emerged from the shadows of the jungle with a whip in hand.

Zamira sent out a mental call for Akia to come and save her; she felt his answering response. They were both still alive, so there was hope. She just had to keep Daemon occupied and distracted until Akia arrived.

Daemon walked over placing the noise canceling ear plugs into his ears. He removed her gag and she coughed for fresh air.

"I'd like you to know that I've had these things modified so I can enjoy your screams but your voice won't be able to mesmerize me." He grinned as he caressed her cheek before slapping her bruised face.

"Well this seems awfully familiar, Daemon. I'm beginning to think you may only be a one note wonder."

Unlike last time, Daemon wasted no time taunting her before landing the first blow of the whip. Zamira cried out as pain burned across her back.

Zamira.

She tried to shut Akia out of her mind as three more blows landed in rapid succession. She didn't want him experiencing this with her. She could feel the blood seeping from the wounds on her back. Daemon decided to walk around her landing blow after blow on every part of her body except her face.

She could feel Akia getting closer, so she knew she had to hold out just a little bit longer. Daemon pulled the ropes holding her arms up until her toes could no longer touch the ground. The pressure on her shoulders was painful by itself, but not being able to brace for the blows of the whip seemed to magnify the pain she felt.

Instinctively she tried to sing her way out of this situation only to have Daemon laugh at her. He had successfully modified his ear plugs to counter her hypnotic voice.

He picked up a secondary whip and with practiced strokes rained down twice as many blows in half the time. Her body was slick with sweat and blood. Her tunic and pants were hanging from her in tatters.

Zamira was having difficulty staying conscious. Somehow she knew that if she couldn't scream to provide Daemon with his entertainment he would just kill her and be done with it. Where was Akia?

Another blow deepened the cut across her stomach. At this rate she would be covered in scars that even a regen unit couldn't fix. That is if she survived. Daemon flicked the long whip around her throat and started to strangle her. She reached for Akia to say good bye.

You live! Damn it to the five hells. You live for me, jinaria. *For Us! I am almost there.*

Daemon loosened the whip around her neck and Zamira gasped for breath. He came up and shoved the handle of the whip under her chin, forcing her to look him in the eyes.

"Defiant as ever I see. But at least I have broken through your cool composure. I wonder how much more you can take before I break you completely."

Zamira spat in Daemon's face. She had power that he had never even conceived of. He was a worm beneath her boot and he didn't even know it. All the rage and hurt bubbled to the surface. The pain she had witnessed, the senseless violence…all because of this man. It would end here…no more would she stand idly by while Daemon Tanis lived.

She closed her eyes and centered herself. The power was deep within her. The last time she let it loose it was instinctual. She had kept this power buried for so long that now she had to dig to find it again. She knew it was there somewhere.

Daemon rained blows down, frustrated that she no longer screamed and cried out in pain. She was beyond pain at this point. She was searching for the dark power buried behind the light of her soul. In her mind she thought she heard Akia's cry of denial as she rode the wave of power back to the surface and her body.

The music was building in her soul. Dark.

Dangerous. Deadly. Daemon's ear plugs wouldn't save him as the tone she would produce wouldn't be heard, only felt. She would stop the rhythm of his heart and he would drop dead just like the flock of colorful birds from her memory. Unlike the birds, Daemon deserved to die.

She snapped her eyes open and opened her mouth to kill the man who had terrorized her entire planet, only to see Akia calmly walking up behind the crazed Daemon. He grabbed the man by the head and with a single quick movement snapped his neck. Daemon looked eternally surprised as his body fell to the ground.

Akia ran to Zamira and lifted her up; he sliced through the ropes and gently untied her hands. She had to force the dark power back into its hiding place before she could even cry out in pain as feeling rushed back into her fingers. She didn't want to possibly injure Akia in the process.

Tears streaked down her face and Akia kissed them away.

"We really need to discuss this habit of yours of getting kidnapped by sadistic madmen."

Zamira laughed and then burst into tears, clinging to Akia's strength.

"I was going to kill him, Akia," she hiccupped. "Why did you stop me?"

Akia brushed the hair from Zamira's face and kissed her gently. "I told you that I am your beast. You are the light to my darkness, the beauty to my ugliness." He placed a finger on her lips as she began to protest that he was not ugly. "I bring death and destruction, you bring love and life. Where would the balance be if we both brought death?"

Zamira was stunned. Akia had listened to her all along. She fell even more in love with him in that moment. She wrapped her arms around his neck and sobbed onto his shoulder. Part of it was from the pain of her wounds, part of it was from relief that they were both still alive.

CHAPTER FORTY-ONE

Akia could have held Zamira like that for hours, but soon his communicator was beeping for his attention.

He used one hand to fish it out while the other still held Zamira.

"Akia."

"This is Rolo, we discovered the slip stream depot."

"Good."

"There's a problem. The slip stream depot was near a magma chamber and the explosion cracked the wall between them. Lava is leaking through the cracks and the place is most likely going to blow soon. A couple of Tanis techs tried to shore up the wall using the pulse shield technology, but they are saying it may hold for a couple of hours at best."

"What are you telling me, Rolo?"

"We need to evacuate now!"

The sounds of battle were heard in the distance. "*Frexing* hells, it is going to be nearly impossible to get the Imperial troops out of here in time."

Zamira stood on shaky legs. "Tell Rolo to open the stasis chambers then get out of there. Get me over to the battle field and I will take care of the rest."

Akia didn't question his mate, he just relayed her orders and scooped her up. He started running towards the battle with her in his arms. At the battle sight she said she needed the high ground. They were able to climb part way up the mountain to a ledge that overlooked the entire battle field. Hundreds of soldiers in Tanis and Imperial uniforms were engaged in combat. Seeing the chaos, Akia wasn't sure she was going to be able to get the troops out in time.

Zamira walked to the edge of the ledge and closed her eyes. She took a deep breath and let out a pure tone that echoed across the landscape. It was the same tone she had used in the arena, and like the arena everyone within hearing distance froze. The she started to sing. Soon everyone below dropped their weapons and began marching towards the mountain lab. The injured were picked up by the able bodied and carried off the field of battle if need be.

While she still sang Akia heard her in his mind: *Call for transports immediately, we have little time to spare.*

Akia did as she asked while Zamira continued to sing. Tanis and Imperial soldiers alike placed the wounded at the mouth of the cavern while they marched in an orderly fashion inside. Soon the soldiers were walking back out leading the naked and confused bodies from the stasis lab. No wonder she wanted Rolo to open the chambers. Soon the clearing in front of the cavern was filled with hundreds of people and still Zamira sang.

The transports arrived and took as many as possible to safety under Akia's directions while the mountain rumbled. And still Zamira sang. The transports returned multiple times until everyone, even the Tanis, were loaded and taken away. And still Zamira sang.

She finally collapsed from exhaustion. Akia carried her down the mountain to catch the last transport with Rolo and the rest of their crew. As they lifted into the air, the mountain shook as an explosion deep within rumbled across the land. Soon lava flowed out of the mouth of the cavern destroying and sealing away the despicable experiments and business of the Tanis.

Daemon was dead. Akia received a report that Batu's reinforcements had arrived and were able to push the enemy out of Ludus Prime space. Now they just needed to figure out what to do with the rest of them here on the ground.

EPILOGUE

Two months later…

"I don't care what the Kassis want, Ghaleb," Zamira said. "Those that were created here have the rights of our citizenry. I will not force them to go to a planet they have never known against their will." Zamira crossed her arms and glared back at the angry monarch on the other side of the holoimage.

"Twice curse you, woman. Do you realize the position you are putting me in as your ally?"

Zamira just smiled. She had met Ghaleb after the final battle against the Tanis. Against Reijo's recommendation, Ghaleb had been on one of the reinforcement ships. She soon discovered that he was more bark than bite when it came to the females in his sphere.

"I'm not saying they can't go, only that I won't force them to leave. Have the Kassis send an ambassador with a contingent of educators to teach these people about their heritage. They are like children, eager to learn."

"Fine, I'll see what I can do." The holoimage clicked off and Zamira heard a chuckle behind her.

"Giving Ghaleb an ulcer again I see."

Zamira smiled and tilted her head up for a kiss which Akia easily obliged.

"It will be good practice for him when he has his own family and children." Zamira turned and laid a hand on Akia's chest. With a shy smile, she looked up at the mountain of a man that she loved. "Speaking of children…"

Akia looked confused and then it dawned on him. "Are you saying what I think you are saying?"

Zamira nodded, "Confirmed this morning by the medics."

Akia picked Zamira up and twirled her around with a whooping holler.

"Put me down, you big lug, unless you want to be wearing my breakfast," she said with a laugh.

He quickly put her down with concerned eyes, "Are you ill? Is everything alright with the baby?"

"I'm fine. It is just morning sickness. It makes me queasy."

Akia caressed her cheek and looked so serious that Zamira reached up for his hand.

"You know that you are my miracle, just like the child you carry. I will always love you."

Zamira smiled and stood up on her tiptoes to kiss his lips. "I will remind you of that when it comes time to change the diapers."

B.D. Snowden is a Texas native living in the Great Plains with her children of both two-legged and four-legged varieties. She is a voracious reader whose book habit literally brought a small town library to life. One day, when she was unable to get something new to read, she started turning the stories floating through her head into concrete concepts on paper.

Find information about new releases and appearances at:

Geekygothblog.wordpress.com

Facebook.com/BrandiceSnowdenWriter

twitter.com/GeekyGOTHcom